TALES FROM *Sourwood Mountain*

NEREID

TESS SERIES - BOOK TWO

by Jenni Lorraine

With love and dedication to my children.

To my childhood best friend, Stefanie.

And to childhood, itself.

May we always out-wit our monsters.

Prologue

When Ellen Dewey got snatched up from the Sonic parking lot, she fought so hard she left her press-on fingernails scattered across the pavement like confetti.

When she'd got there to work her shift that afternoon, she was running late on account of her brother, Brian Dewey, parking behind her car in the driveway and then taking his time moving his truck to let her out.

Brian was always doing stuff like that to Erin. That's how come she hated it that her mama was always making her help him out with stuff.

Brian was two years older than Ellen, but had never acted like it. She was seventeen and had been working at the Sonic since she was fourteen. Brian had never worked a day in his life, but would always show up at closing time begging her for free french fries.

"You're just gonna throw 'em in the trash anyway!" he'd say. If Ellen told him that she couldn't give him any fries because they didn't have extra, he'd always come back with, "Well who's gonna know if you drop in a handful right now?"

They were different in just about every way you could imagine. Ellen was born beautiful. She was tall, blonde, blue-eyed, and leggy. All the boys in Adelaide swarmed her, even though she never really paid any of them much mind.

Brian, on the other hand, was tubby, greasy, short, and pimpled. Somehow, though, he still always managed to have a girlfriend.

My mama once theorized that Brian had such good luck with the ladies because of who their daddy, Paul Dewey, was.

Paul had been in charge of Felicity Holdings, the "big bank" in Adelaide, for as long as he'd been out of college, I guess. He'd gone off to some fancy school after he graduated from Adelaide High School, got some sparkly degree, and came back to take over the bank when his grandfather retired from running it before him.

Charlie never put his money in there. He said that he didn't trust any financial institution that had been run by the same damned family ever since Jesus was breathing. He especially hated the idea because the Deweys were one of the richest families in Adelaide as a result of their ties to the bank.

"There's something fishy about a family that keeps getting richer and richer running a bank in a town full of poor folk," Charlie'd say- and he was right! Sheila Dewey, Paul's wife, had never worked a day in her life, either, so all the money had to be coming in on Paul's paychecks.

They lived in what seemed like a mansion to me. If you drove south out of Adelaide on the highway, you'd see it way on up in the hills, like a castle looking down on everyone. If it was early morning or coming up close to dark, the sun would hit all the windows and reflect off and it looked like a golden palace.

The house was as big as the elementary school, easily, and made almost entirely of wooden logs and double sided windows. The outside was mirrored glass, of course, so nobody could see in- but once they did a tour of homes in Adelaide for a charity thing and Mama took me along and we got to see the inside of the Dewey house.

It was all marble countertops and plush white carpeting and sparkling ceramic tile. What I remember most, though, was Ellen's room.

Ellen's room was painted pastel pink with cream carpeting and a fluffy bedspread and so many pillows on the bed I didn't know where she found room to sleep, herself! She had a little desk with a computer on it, too. Her own computer!

Next to the desk was a shelf full of books.

"This is Ellen's room," Sheila said, motioning around- her big, cheesy fake smile spread from ear to ear. "As you can see, she's our reader. She wants to be a book writer some day!"

It was the strangest thing I think I'd ever heard- Ellen Dewey wanted to write books? Gorgeous, super model Ellen Dewey was a *nerd*? It made absolutely no sense.

Predictably, Brian's room was the opposite. It was dark and cluttered with a big television set and every game console imaginable hooked up to it.

"Pardon the mess in here," Sheila said, embarrassed when she looked around. "I asked him to clean it, but you know how teenage boys are."

She shuffled us out of there pretty quick, but not before I got a good look at all the half-naked lady posters he had covering his walls. It was always clear to me - even as a little girl- that Brian had little to no respect for women. Not his mother. Not his sister. Not anyone else.

I have always assumed that was part of the reason Brian was always begging free fries off his sister. He could certainly afford to buy them if he was hungry, but it wasn't so much about the fries, but about harassing her at a job he didn't understand her wanting and making her serve him in an environment where he felt he had some kind of upper hand.

Had it not been for this unusual tradition, though, there's no telling how long it might have taken for anyone to notice Ellen gone.

It was Brian that first noticed something was out of sorts on the night Ellen vanished. He'd made his way up to the Sonic, as usual, to beg for his helping of free fries. When he got there, he didn't see Ellen anywhere.

"Candace!" he hollered out the window of his pick-up. "Where's my sister?"

Candace was one of the other girls who worked at the Sonic. She wasn't nearly as pretty as Ellen, but she got her own share of attention from boys. Erik's brothers said it was because she wasn't the type of girl that ever said no to anybody.

"She took off!" Candace said. "I reckon she got sick of the shit around here and just quit! About an hour ago, she got yelled at in the kitchen over something and took a tray of food out the door to a customer and just didn't come back."

Brian gestured behind the building. "Her car's still here," he said. "How could she have left without her car?"

Candace shrugged. "Maybe she went for a walk? You aren't even supposed to be coming around here anymore at closing time, anyway! That's probably what she was in trouble for was you coming and getting free food all the time. She probably left so she wouldn't have to see your face!"

Brian scoffed at her and shook his head. "Well then I guess I'll just have to do something else to piss her off," he said. He climbed out of his truck and headed back toward where her car was parked.

She had a pretty little white Mustang, bought for her by her Daddy, of course. It had fuzzy pink seat covers and vanity plates that read "Ell3N" and a princess tiara decal in the back window.

As Brian came up to the car, he reached for his pocket knife. His intent was to carve something ugly into that vinyl decal, but the closer he got to the car, he started to realize something was amiss.

Her driver's side door wasn't shut all the way and her key was in the ignition, although the car had not been started. Her name tag and purse were laying in the passenger side seat.

And right there on the ground- right next to the car door, surrounded by press-on-nail confetti, laid both her white roller skates, splattered with what looked like fresh blood.

Chapter One

My mouth was full of Big League Chew bubble gum, but it did nothing to slow my speech.

"The Nereids are like mermaids and they hate it when anyone else is more beautiful than them!" I explained emphatically. "And that's how come they started a new rule that if someone didn't sacrifice all the pretty girls to them, then they were going to do bad things. So people sometimes have to throw all the prettiest girls into the sea to keep them from causing all kinds of other problems! Get it?!"

Alan was barely listening. He was sitting at his desk, resting his forehead in one hand as he read over the witness statements from Ellen's disappearance. He stopped, giving me one of his best *you-can't-be-serious* looks, then scratched his head.

"Do you hear yourself, girl?" he asked. "You just said these mermaid things live in the sea. We're talking about Pichol Creek being where Ruby was found and there ain't no telling yet where Ellen's gone. For all we know, she got a nosebleed and took off with some friends for a few days."

"Just because some live in the sea doesn't

mean that others can't live in the creek!" I quipped back. "Think about it- TWO pretty girls go missing in the same town? And it's a town where there's monsters living everywhere! The only thing that makes sense is Nereids. Someone's throwin' pretty girls down in the creek to save the town from whatever bad things they say they're goin' to do. We need to figure out who is doing that and then they can tell us where to find the Nereids and that's where Ellen will be, I bet!"

Alan shook his head and looked up at the clock. Mama and Charlie were visiting Joel in the jailhouse and had thirty minutes to talk to him. I said I wanted to stay and visit with Alan, which they didn't really like, but didn't argue about, either. I had to tell him about the Nereids in Pichol Creek so that he could find the real culprit behind Ruby and let Joel come home.

"Joel didn't do it, that's one thing we do know for sure!" I said. "If Joel did it, then how come Ellen's missing now and Joel was already in jail when she disappeared? That doesn't make any sense."

"Maybe it's two different people," Alan said. "I don't know that the same person got both girls."

I scoffed. "Two girl snatchers in Adelaide?" I asked. "Are you kiddin' me? We don't even have one Chuck E Cheese."

Alan slammed his papers down on his desk and heaved a heavy sigh. "Tessie, I appreciate you coming down here and telling me what you know, but I need to be focusing on this work."

"We are doing work!" I said. "We are solving this case together and I'm telling you how we are going to do it."

"You'll be a good lawyer someday," he said. "But right now, I need you to please leave my office. I love visiting with you. You're a good kid. I am not mad at you. I just cannot listen to all this anymore and I can't really talk about it with you, either. I can't even talk to grown people about most of this until I know what I'm dealing with!"

"Nereids," I said. "You're dealing with Nereids. And I know it's hard to talk to grown-ups about it because grown-ups don't really like to believe in stuff like that. Trust me. I get it. But we don't have to tell them! We just have to figure out who put Ruby in the creek. That person will already know!"

"Please leave my office," Alan said again, pleading as he leaned back in his chair and threw his head back, gazing at the ceiling.

I looked at the clock. There was about ten minutes left before Mama and Charlie would be done talking to Joel.

"Can I have a Coke?" I asked, eyeing the little fridge next to Alan's desk. It was hot outside and I didn't want to wait out there thirsty.

"You can have any damned thing you want if it means you'll shut your mouth and get out of here," he said.

It should have offended me. It did not. I was just happy to get my hands on a cold cola.

I sprung to my feet and helped myself to one, then went outside. I sat down on a bench at the station entrance and looked down the road, where a bunch of kids from school were playing hopscotch on the sidewalk. I recognized one of them as Kimberly Carel from my grade.

I waved at her. "Hi, Kimberly!" I hollered. She looked up at me and waved back. Just as she did, her mother walked out of the drug store and turned her head to see me. She put her hand on Kimberly's shoulder and guided her away, scolding her about talking to me.

I couldn't hear it, but I could tell. There's a face Mamas pull when they are mad at their kids for stupid reasons that they know are stupid reasons. It's a combination of self righteousness mixed with just a tiny bit of embarrassment because they know they're not acting like a grown up oughta act. Mama got that look on her face a lot- usually when she would be telling me to mind my business about things like always having money for hair dye and make-up but not for push pops from the Schwan's truck.

There's also a way kids act when they know they're being scolded for something they ought not be scolded for. Their shoulders slump and they drag their feet a little more. They bite their lips and fume extra. That's what Kimberly was doing.

I was pretty well used to it all, though. If that summer so far had taught me anything at all, it was that sometimes, even when you're not, you're going to be called a bad person by someone. It was happening to Joel and it was happening to me and the rest of our family, too.

Since Joel was arrested, I was having a hard time getting anyone to come play with me. Even Debbie had stopped bringing Christopher out to the house as much. The same sort of things were happening all over town to Mama and Charlie, too.

It seemed everyone had made up their mind that Joel was a killer and that we were all the family of a killer. They acted like we'd been covering up for him all that time and that we were nothing but trouble makers.

Even people at Mama's work had quit sitting with her in the breakroom, she said.

She didn't tell me that, directly, of course. I had heard her crying about it to Charlie after I went to bed one night.

Even though I heard him tell Mama it would all blow over and get better soon, it still hurt her feelings. It hurt mine, too.

I missed my friends. I missed Joel. I missed just having things be easy.

The only way to get back to that, though, would be to prove Joel didn't do it.

And that meant I had to start hunting some Nereids.

Chapter Two

It wasn't as clear to Alan what was going on in Adelaide. He was still running with the assumption that both girls had been taken at the hands of separate men- and that Ruby had been killed by Joel.

This, of course, created quite a bit of gossip throughout the town. On one hand, nobody wanted to doubt our sheriff. On the other, nobody wanted to believe that there were multiple villains running amok in Adelaide.

It was different this time, though. The first scary story had centered around the skeleton of a long-dead girl that nobody had even noticed was missing. This time, there was a race against the clock in the hopes that he might be able to save one that could still be alive somewhere. Not only that, but she was a Dewey: Adelaide royalty as far as anyone around town was concerned.

The good news was that, being fresh, there was a whole lot more evidence to follow than what Ruby's case had to offer. Joel started his investigation with a look at surveillance video from the Sonic drive-in.

The problem with the surveillance video, though, was that it was summer time in Virginia- and that meant the orbweaver spiders were out in force. One had built a web right in front of that camera lens, which was dirty and old anyway. The footage was also in black and white.

All Alan could really make out of the video was that, at the time Ellen vanished, there was an early-80s model Chevy Scottsdale pickup parked next to Ellen's car in the parking lot. On the video, the truck appeared to be a light gray, but not white. So Alan knew he was hunting one that was brightly colored. The license plates were muddy and he couldn't make them out.

Right off the top of his head, he knew of three brightly colored Scottsdales, though: Charlie had a red Scottsdale, a local drunk by the name of Edgar Hollis had a tan one, and Steve Merrill had a light blue one.

Of the three, Edgar was the only one with a teenage son. Edgar's son, Jimmy, was a pitcher and captain of the Adelaide Waterbucks high school baseball team.

I had never understood why our high school chose the Waterbuck as a mascot, since there wasn't such a thing in Virginia. I'd looked it up in an encyclopedia at the library once and found that the waterbuck was some kind of African antelope with long pointed horns.

It wasn't even particularly formidable like some wild animals that get thrown on high school jerseys might be. A tiger or a bear will eat you. An eagle is King of the skies.

A waterbuck is pretty much just a stinkin' goat. While I didn't understand the selection, I ultimately figured it was apt enough for Adelaide.

And Waterbuck Captain was certainly an appropriate title for the likes of Jimmy Hollis.

Jimmy was tall, lanky, and pimple-faced. Jimmy's mama, Janice, was somehow still married to Edgar, despite Edgar's unsavory reputation around town and they lived with their three kids- seventeen-year-old Jimmy, thirteen-year-old Jackie, and six-year-old Dalton- in a duplex just up the road from Rowdy's in a neighborhood the locals called Tangerine Town.

Tangerine Town got its name because of the Morningside Motel. The motel was painted orange and yellow and apparently had been a real nice place when it first popped up back in the 50s. By the mid-90s, though, the rooms had become extended-stay units that were occupied mostly by drug addicts, felons, and girls that walked up and down the road in next-to-nothing outfits. Mama said they went on dates with boys to get money or drugs.

Of all the places around that Mama and Charlie ever told us to stay away from, Tangerine Town topped the list- and it was the one place I never even thought about trying to go. I didn't want to. Everyone I knew who lived over that way was despicable.

Admittedly, I didn't know the Hollises well. Their kids were either too old or too young for me to worry about, but if they lived in Tangerine Town, I knew they were bad.

That's why I didn't think anything of it that day when Mama and Charlie finally came out to the truck so we could head home and Mama said she'd overheard Alan on the phone asking where he might find Edgar.

"You reckon Edgar had something to do with this Ellen business?" Mama asked Charlie.

"Hell, Jolene!" Charlie said. "That man probably has to call Edgar Hollis ten times a week. Let's not get ahead of ourselves here!"

"Well he does have that boy Ellen's age," Mama said. "What's that boy's name, Tessie?"

"Jimmy," I said. "Kids at school call him Gimme Jimmy because he's always trying to get girls to give him kisses and stuff. He's weird."

"Well there you go," Mama said. "I bet he's involved with Ellen." She shook her head with a sigh.

"He'd have been no bigger than a piss ant when Ruby got done in," Charlie said. "If the same one has got them both, it doesn't make sense it'd be Jimmy Hollis."

A still fell over the truck. Charlie, of course, was hoping for a miracle- hoping that, somehow, both girls would be proven to have been taken by the same man because that would prove Joel's innocence.

"What did Joel's lawyer say?" I asked, cutting the quiet. "Is Joel going to get to come home?"

"He has a hearing coming up next week," Mama said. "Right now it looks like they're going to try to charge him, but it will be up to the judge to decide if any of the evidence is enough to do that."

Charlie scoffed. "Evidence," he sneered. "What have they got, really? That he planted some flowers? That she was pregnant and cheating on him with Dickie? None of that means jack shit except he got his feelings all tied up in a messy woman. We've all done that. I bet Sheriff Alan Cline, himself, has been in some right messes, too."

"It's the ax, Charlie," Mama said. "That damned dog's blood on the ax. They're trying to say he's the one that killed Job and that he did that because Job dug her up."

"You know and I know he wouldn't have killed Tessie's dog," Charlie said, his voice growing stern as he cut his eyes down at me then back up at her. "And they can't prove that it's Job's blood. He told them about that rabid mongrel he took care of. Hell, half the town can remember when he did it. Remember?"

The truck got quiet again, but only for a moment.

"Whatever happens, Tessie, you remember that. Joel didn't kill your dog, you hear me?" he asked.

I nodded.

"I'm sorry we found the skeleton," I said. "If I'd never found that, Joel wouldn't be in trouble. It was better when we all just thought she ran away."

Charlie shook his head.

"It'll be better yet when the son of a bitch that did it is where he belongs. Have faith, little girl. God's not gonna let this one play out like this for long. They'll get him."

I thought of the Nereids swimming in Pichol Creek, smirking. I thought of bubbles carrying the sound of their laughter from underwater up to the surface, bursting at the top as the woods filled with the thrown chorus of sinister giggles.

I wanted to believe Charlie.

But thousands of years had passed and God hadn't stopped those monsters yet.

Chapter Three

The very next morning, I woke up and found Alan Cline sitting at our kitchen table with Mama and Charlie. Charlie looked mad. Mama looked like she always did when entertaining a guest- pleasant, but ready for it to be over.

"If you're asking where I was the night Ellen disappeared, I was right here calling every defense lawyer I could think of in the county trying to get my brother out of jail," Charlie said.

Alan put his hands up as if calming a crowd, despite only the four of us being in the room.

"Now, Charlie, I'm not accusing you of anything," he said. "I am just saying that I need to ask you some questions because a truck like yours was there the night Ellen got taken. You know how it is. I have to follow every lead."

"A truck like mine?" Charlie asked. "A truck just like mine? How good's that picture you got of it? Can you see the scratch on my hood? You see the decal Tessie gave me for Christmas last year on the back window? What is that decal a picture of? You know that?"

It was a rattlesnake, but I wasn't going to answer out loud. I got it out of a vending machine at Pizza Hut when we all went shopping in Roanoke.

"I reckon I didn't look hard enough and it's black and white video," Alan sighed. "All I know is it's a lighter or bright colored Scottsdale about the same year as yours."

"You know how many Scottsdales there are in Adelaide?" Charlie fumed. "Can't drive down Main Street and not see one. Hell, how many do you think there are in all of Virginia? That girl got taken from a fast food joint. It could have been any grifter that rolled in off the highway!"

Alan wasn't talking anymore. He was just nodding. He knew he'd made a mistake coming to try to talk to Charlie with Joel still behind bars.

"I guess it's better evidence than you have against Joel, though," Charlie kept on. "You don't even know what kind of vehicle Ruby last got into, do you? My brother's locked up suspected of murder because you found dog blood on an ax."

He huffed, shaking his head then reached frantically into his jacket pocket for his cigarettes.

"I'm sorry, Jo," he said. "I gotta smoke a damned cigarette. This beats all I've ever heard."

"I know you're mad at me over your brother, Charlie," Alan said. "I promise you I wouldn't have him locked up if I didn't have a real strong reason to believe he's the one that hurt Ruby. I can't let you in on everything I know, but I took a trip to Nashville. I know some things about Ruby and Dickie that would have rightfully pissed Joel off. Any man would have lost his temper with her."

"Not Joel," Charlie said. "Joel loved that girl

more than I've ever seen him love anyone. He knew
what kind of person she was. He cried over it more
times than I can count- but when she left for
Nashville, that was the end of it. He really thought
that's where she'd gone and that she just didn't want
to speak to him anymore. It took him a long time to
get over it. A man doesn't grieve like he did if they
have all the answers they want. He couldn't figure out
why she hadn't ever called him. Now we all know."

Alan looked at me apologetically, as if he knew
what he was about to say would break my heart,
despite being unavoidable.

"How sure are you that the blood on that ax
wasn't Tessie's dog?" he asked. "The rabid dog makes
sense, but all the use of that ax since then ought to
have worn that blood away by now."

"That's it!" Mama said, standing up and
scooting her chair back. "Alan, I'm going to ask you to
leave right now. That's too far! Not in front of my little
girl."

"Because you think it could be, Jo," Alan said,
clearly clued in by her response. "Charlie, your wife
thinks he killed the dog- doesn't that make you
wonder?"

Mama didn't correct him. She just turned and
ushered me out of the kitchen.

It didn't take long before Charlie and Alan
finished whatever words they were exchanging and I
saw Alan walk past the window, having exited the
other doorway. He got in his car and left. I, of course,

bolted right back to the table to listen in on the fussing.

"I cannot believe he came into our home and said something like that," Mama said. Her eyes were watering. It was rare to see her so angry she cried.

"He had no right," Charlie said.

Just then, he turned to me as if he suddenly remembered that I had overheard the worst parts of the conversation.

"You can't take everything he said to heart, Tessie," he cautioned. "We all know Joel and that means we all know he'd never hurt anybody. Definitely not anyone he loved. Not Ruby or you. He knows how much you loved that dog. Right, Mama?"

She looked turned back toward me, too, wiping the tears from her eyes.

And she hesitated.

"Right," she finally answered. "Joel wouldn't ever do anything to hurt you, Tessie."

But she didn't say he wouldn't hurt Job. Charlie hadn't said it, either. There was something they both knew and were holding back.

"Did Joel like Job, Mama?" I asked, trying to afford her an opportunity to say what was on her mind.

"Yes," she said in the same put-on voice as

before. "Joel liked Job just fine, Sweetheart."

He didn't, though. It was something I hadn't realized until right at that moment- but the tone of Mama's voice was telling the story.

I needed to know more.

"Did Job ever do things that made Joel mad? Was Joel mad that Job found Ruby?"

There was a chill in the kitchen as both grown ups sat quiet.

Finally, Charlie broke through the silence.

"When people are hurting, they look for things to be mad at," he said. "Joel was upset that Job gnawed on Ruby. He wasn't mad that he found her."

And there it was.

The truth about the bloody ax.

I had never been so upset that I felt dizzy before.

I let out an awful squall, then ran up the stairs and slammed the door to my bedroom before I flopped onto the mattress. The volume of it woke up Mallory and she started screaming, too, but nobody scolded me.

They had no right.

Chapter Four

By the next day, I'd already thought it over and decided that I would have to forgive Joel for what he'd done to Job, even if it meant I'd never forget it.

He was family and I loved him - and I understood why he was upset, although I couldn't make sense of the violence he'd put behind it. Not until I thought about how angry I'd been when I thought the tailypo had done it. I'd wanted to kill that tailypo. I'd wanted to see it suffer.

There was no way to know who had hurt Ruby and laid her in that grave, but Job had sunk his teeth into her skull. Like Charlie said, hurt people look for things to be mad at.

Job was the obvious choice.

Joel loved Ruby. He loved her so much it made everyone around them sick from hearing and watching it.

Just because he'd hurt Job didn't mean he could have hurt her- and that's what I intended to tell Alan when I got to the station.

Mama was real queasy with morning sickness and still in her bed.

Charlie had run off to meet with some lawyer about Joel's case and about Alan coming into our house the day before and making such a scene.

Nana Carter was in the rocking chair in the living room watching the morning news.

"I'm going to ride my bike to town, Nana," I said. "I'll probably be home by lunchtime."

She stopped mid rock and turned toward me, cocking one eyebrow.

"What are you going to do in town?" she asked.

Nana had never questioned me before.

"I think I'll go see if Christopher wants to play, maybe?" I offered, shrugging my shoulders. "I'm just tired of being here."

Nana nodded thoughtfully. "I don't know that I should let you go alone," she said. "A lot of bad things are happening around here lately and we don't know who snatched up that girl, yet."

I scoffed. "Look at me, Nana," I said. "I'm not Ellen Dewey. Nobody's going to grab me up."

She chuckled as she laid her head back, resting it against the chair.

"Come here," she said. "Bring me my purse."

I grabbed her purse off the table and carried it to her. She reached inside and counted out a handful of quarters, then dropped them into my jacket pocket, zipping it shut.

"You call me every thirty minutes until you get home," she said, sternly. "When you get to the last of our quarters, it's time to head back."

I nodded. "I will, Nana." I promised.

She gave me a tight hug, planted a kiss on my forehead, and sent me on my way.

I rode in relative peace and quiet until I passed the trailer park. I wanted to stop and see if Christopher was home, just like I said I'd do. I hated knowing I'd lied to Nana, but I was on a secret mission that she couldn't know about.

I had tried to tell Joel about the Nereids before, but he didn't listen. Today, I'd make him.

I turned east on the busy street after the trailer park and that's the first time I noticed the gray car following me. It turned when I did and drove slow, as if it didn't want to pass me or even come up too close. It gave me an uneasy feeling, so I turned against my better judgment toward the golf course, taking me away from the sheriff's station.

The car turned behind me again.

Maybe they're just going this way, I thought to myself, trying my hardest not to panic.

I made one more quick, unexpected turn down a residential boulevard. It was a part of town I was unfamiliar with.

The car turned behind me again- and that's

when I realized I had nowhere to go.

I was stuck in a cul de sac.

Out of options, I stopped my bike outside a window where I saw a TV running inside. A woman was sitting in a recliner, watching the TV as she talked on the telephone.

I prepared to scream louder than I ever had as I watched the gray car pull slowly up in front of me and come to a stop. The tinted driver's side window rolled down automatically and the pretty woman inside flashed me a toothy grin.

"You seem a little lost, Darlin'!" she said.

"Are you following me?" I asked, relieved to see a woman. I didn't know an awful lot about kidnappers- but I knew that most of them were men.

She giggled. "You caught me," she said. "I saw you coming in from out of town. Are you Jolene Bradley's little girl?"

I nodded. "It's Jolene Westpoole now, though," I said. "She got married again."

"That's right!" she said. "I just wanted to meet you. I hear you're a big monster hunter! Is that what you're doing out today?"

I shook my head. "Not specifically," I answered. "I'm always hunting monsters, but today I'm doing other stuff, too."

She smiled. "Ah," she said. "I see."

It got quiet for a minute. Uncomfortably quiet. I needed to fill the silence with noise, so I decided to tell her about Nereids.

"I'm actually going to go see the Sheriff because I think the two missing girls were both taken by Nereids," I blurted out. "That's a kind of mermaid. They get jealous of pretty girls so they tell people they need to throw the pretty girls in the water for them or they'll do bad stuff."

"Right," she said, nodding her head. "That makes sense, actually! Both the missing girls were very pretty, weren't they?"

I nearly broke the skin around my mouth smiling so wide. Someone was finally hearing me!

"Yes!" I said. "And at least one of them we know was in the water because her bones were in Pichol Creek."

"Exactly!" she said. "You found those bones, didn't you?"

"My dog did," I said. My heart sank at the thought of Job finding the bones. It was the event that ended his life, after all.

I don't know why I felt so comfortable telling the strange woman in the car about it. Perhaps I just needed to tell someone to make my little heart feel better.

"You know my uncle loved Ruby- that's the girl that we found," I said. "And he got really mad at my dog and he killed him because he chewed on her bones, but he lied to the sheriff and said he killed some other dog because he was scared. But the sheriff really doesn't believe that and he thinks my uncle killed my dog because he found Ruby and that my uncle killed Ruby, too, and I need to tell the sheriff all of this so he'll let my uncle go. It's a big misunderstanding!"

I heard my voice breaking and felt the tears welling in my eyes. I made myself stop talking so I wouldn't embarrass myself crying out in the open.

"Well," the lady said. "I don't think you oughta go telling the sheriff anything. I think if he finds out that your uncle killed that dog for sure, he's going to see it just as more proof of his idea. You better just not say anything about that to him, at all."

I realized she was probably right.

"I just want to help Joel come home," I said. "I'm mad he killed my dog, but I still love him. It was awful what he did to Job, really. Part of me wanted him to stay in jail just for that. It was so bad when I found Job that Pearline the witch had to save me and that's the day I found out I'm a witch, too. Did you know that? That I'm a witch? We're white witches, me and Pearline. That means we aren't bad. You don't have to be scared of us."

She shook her head. "No, Honey," she said. "I didn't know that."

I nodded. "I don't have strong powers, though," I said. "Not yet, anyway. I don't know how to help. I just know that I want to help. Do you understand me?"

I felt my voice break again and tears welling in my eyes. It was too late to stop them this time, though. The woman in the car reached for my hand and gave it a tight squeeze.

"Don't tell the sheriff anything," she said. "That's how you help. Your uncle will be home soon."

"How do you know?" I asked.

She smiled.

"Because I'm a white witch, too."

Chapter Five

Of course, I had no way of knowing who I was talking to that day- but it would turn out that her name was Detective Kathleen Quinn and she worked for the Virginia Bureau of Criminal Investigation.

She'd been following the events in Adelaide closely ever since Ruby's body was found, overseeing Alan's investigation from afar. When he arrested Joel, another detective had come in from Richmond to talk to him, but hadn't got any further than Alan had with information.

When Kathleen read those reports, she couldn't believe what she was looking at and drove all the way to Adelaide on her own to talk to Alan about what he'd done wrong.

Kathleen was a gorgeous woman. She was tall, with dark brown curly hair, fair skin, and the bluest eyes I'd ever seen.

In truth, Kathleen was pushing forty years old, but most who looked at her would have had a hard time believing she was even thirty. She'd never been married or had children of her own, but not because she didn't want to. Her personal life had just always taken a back seat to her work, and it seemed like there was always more work to do than she knew how to handle.

When she walked into the sheriff's station that day, all the deputies stopped and looked at her with their jaws hanging onto the floor. They didn't know who she was, but they were sure glad she'd decided to come in there and see them.

"Can I help you, Ma'am?" one of them asked, scrambling to be the first to talk to her.

"Yes, Sir," she said. "I'm looking for Sheriff Alan Cline. Is he in?"

The deputies cut their eyes around at each other nervously before one of them waved her to follow him, then led her back to Alan's office.

"Sir?" he said. "There's a young lady here to see you."

Alan didn't look up from the stack of papers on his desk.

"If it's Tessie, tell her I'm busy," he grumbled.

Kathleen chuckled. "It's me," she said.

Alan's head popped up in disbelief of the voice he'd just heard.

"Kathy!" he said, sliding his chair back. A smile spread across his face. "It's been a long time, Girl! What are you doing here?"

"I got assigned to your kidnapping," she said. "I've been reading the case files. Interesting mess you've got going on here."

Alan sighed.

"I firmly believe it's two separate messes," he started to explain.

"Well I'm not so sure," she answered, not letting him continue. "I'm also not so sure having Joel Westpoole locked up in your jail is the brilliant career move you believe it to be right at this moment."

"Sit down," Alan instructed, motioning toward the extra chair in his office. "I'll explain all this to you."

Kathleen smiled, shaking her head as she took a seat. "I actually already spoke to one of the other investigators," she teased.

"What other investigator?" Alan asked.

"Tessie Rowe," Kathleen smirked. "She's a bright one, Alan. How'd you get so lucky to come by her?"

Alan shook his head, rolling his eyes. "Luck wouldn't be the word," he said.

"You know, she knows that it was her dog that Joel killed," Kathleen offered. "She was on her way here to tell you that. I told her not to say a word to you about it and sent her home, but I'm telling you- that girl knows he killed her dog, but does not believe he killed Ruby Milton. I don't, either."

"What makes you think he didn't do it?" Alan asked. "Ruby, I mean. What makes you think a man capable of chopping a dog his family loved apart with an ax wouldn't end the life of a woman he was scorned by?"

"I don't believe he knew he'd been scorned," Kathleen said. "Whatever defense attorney he gets is going to make the same argument. That's where you're messing up big here, Alan. If this thing goes to trial, you cannot prove beyond a reasonable doubt that he did this- and that's all it takes. Reasonable doubt."

"That's where you're wrong," Alan said. "She was pregnant- possibly with another man's baby. She'd lied about why she was going to Nashville. She'd cheated on him and had no intentions of staying with him and he was obsessed with her. He planted lilies all over the forest after he buried her out there. He killed that dog because it dug her up. It's unreasonable to believe anything else."

"Why'd Dickie kill himself?" Kathleen asked. "This girl gets found and you find out about their relationship, then he kills himself. What's that telling you, Alan? What do the people around town think of it?"

"Dickie had a lifetime of problems.." Joel started to explain.

She cut him off again.

"And this Monte character? You know he's a sexual deviant. He's out there in the woods doing God knows what- the whole town is afraid to leave their women and children around him and he's less than a mile from where her body showed up? Come on, Alan! This case is a defense attorney's goldmine!"

Alan didn't say anything more. He leaned back

in his chair, rubbing his hands all over his face. The stress of the conversation was beginning to get to him.

"Why are you in such a hurry?" Kathleen asked. "What is it about this case that has you sprinting to file it closed?"

Alan grunted, clearing his throat as tears welled in his eyes. He motioned for Kathleen to shut the door and she did as asked.

At the clicking of the door latch, he took a long, deep breath and looked her in the face.

"Tessie Rowe was no taller than this desk the day she watched her daddy raping and beating her mama. She tried to fight him off of her and got chased around through the snow and at the end of that, she watched as her mother picked up a rifle and blew him off the back porch. There was no telephone. Jo sent her to get Charlie Westpoole to call for help."

His voice broke. He leaned forward, resting his face in his hands and took a deep breath before he continued.

"That kid hunts monsters in the woods because she is trying her damndest to believe that people can't do bad things. Death and blood and gore are only as scary as the monsters that cause them and monsters have rules. They only do bad things at night. They only do bad things in the water. They can't come into your house... Tessie has a monster in her house and doesn't know it. Again. And I want to get rid of it before she's old enough to see an ounce more of bloodshed."

Kathleen paused, taking in all of what Alan had told her.

"What if it's you?" she finally asked. "What if her Uncle Joel is an innocent man and the monster in Tessie's life that's come to rob her of something's you, Alan? What then?"

Chapter Six

Charlie beat me home that morning, and it didn't seem like the lawyer had given much good news. He and Mama had already started fighting again by the time I came through the door.

"He needs to just explain why he killed Job," Mama said. "They've got him up there because they think he's lying about everything. If he talks about what he was thinking- as crazy as it may be- it'll at least show some cooperation. He can come home!"

Charlie laughed. "You really think it's going to be that simple? They get him talking about one thing and they're gonna lay into him until they've got him talking about something else. You know how these things go. Joel's not much of a talker anyhow. He's a smartass and his mouth will dig him a deeper hole."

"Well he didn't kill Ruby," Mama said. "How are they going to squeeze something out of him that he didn't do?"

"Have you been watching the news, woman?" Charlie asked. "Just last year over in Arkansas they got three boys to cop to murders they didn't do. Cops don't always play fair and our brains don't always work through shit like this the way we think they should. The best thing for Joel to do right now is keep his damned mouth shut."

Mama sighed, heavy. Then she turned and noticed that I was standing in the room.

"Tessie, you're not supposed to be listening in on all this grown-up talk," she said. She stood up, clearing the coffee cups off the table to wash them.

There was a long silence in the room as both did their best not to talk in front of me anymore.

Charlie lost conviction first.

"Besides, he's already told them he killed that other dog," he said. "If he sticks to that story, they can't disprove it."

"That's not true!" Mama said, spinning around. "At least I don't think it is! I saw something on television just the other night that they can take blood from a crime scene and figure out which person it came from now. They don't match blood types anymore, Charlie! They can put your blood in a machine and see exactly who you are! Why couldn't they do the same with a dog? They had the damned medical examiner come look at Job, remember? They probably have samples of his blood in a bottle somewhere!"

Charlie shook his head, rolling his eyes. "You think too much, woman," he said.

I needed to say something.

"You really don't have to worry about it, Mama," I started. "I met someone in town and she told me that Joel would be out soon."

Both of them stopped talking to each other and proceeded to stare me down.

"Who did you meet in town?" Charlie asked.

I tried to remember if she'd ever told me her name, and ultimately I decided that she hadn't.

"Some white witch," I shrugged. "She followed me on my bike for a while and then when I stopped she started talking to me about Joel and Ruby and you all. She asked me a few questions and we talked about monsters and then she said not to worry because Joel was going to get out soon."

They looked at each other. Palpable confusion filled the room.

Then Mama had a conniption.

"Don't you *ever* talk to *nobody* about any of this!" she said. "Especially not some stranger on the street! And what are you doing stopping and talking to anyone that's been following you on your bicycle?!"

Charlie had a cooler head, but he was just as furious. I could see the veins on his neck starting to pop out.

"What have we told you about talking to strangers, Tessie?" he asked.

"Not to," I said, shrugging my shoulders. "But if I don't ever talk to a stranger, how am I ever going to make new friends?"

That was the wrong thing to say.

"Do not sass Charlie!" Mama said. "You know exactly what he means. That person you talked to could have been anyone, Tessie." Mama's eyes darted back and forth as her head tried to understand who might have wanted to talk to me and who would be asking questions about Joel.

"It could have been a kidnapper!" she carried on. "Or a police officer trying to trick you into saying something bad about him.. Or a.. a.."

Suddenly, her face turned milky white. She looked at Charlie, aghast.

"Do you think it was a reporter?" she asked. "Maybe some big time reporter from the city? Do you think they're getting ready to railroad Joel on the news?"

Her voice shook as she said it. Her hands started shaking, too, and she sat down.

"If she said what she said to Tessie, I reckon not," Charlie said. "Seems like she knows something nobody else knows yet if she's so set on Joel being let out. We need to calm down, Jo. It might not even be a bad thing."

"Right," I said. "It could be a good thing."

Charlie looked at me sternly.

I knew I needed to shut up.

"Tessie," Mama said, burying her face in her hands. "You cannot be talking to anyone about anything that goes on out here- especially not about this case, do you understand?"

"She wasn't asking anything bad!" I argued. "Besides- all anyone wants to know is about this case. That's all anyone is talking about when they talk about us! Who am I going to talk to if I can't talk to anyone that ain't curious about it!"

"You keep your mouth shut or you stay home," Charlie said, sternly. "Those are your only two options."

I didn't say anything. I didn't agree nor disagree.

If staying quiet was Joel's best defense, then I guessed it'd be mine, too.

Chapter Seven

Kathleen, on the other hand, was ready to talk. Specifically, she was ready to talk to Monte.

The day after she nearly got me grounded for the rest of eternity, she showed up bright and early to the sheriff's station with an extra cup of coffee in hand ready to plead her case to Alan.

"What's this?" Alan asked, turning his nose up at the styrofoam cup as she slid it across his desk.

"Cappuccino," she said. "It won't kill you, I promise."

Alan grunted. "Thanks?" he teased. "I have a coffee machine here. Could've saved yourself some time and money."

"When's the last time it was cleaned?" she asked, cocking an eyebrow in his direction.

He didn't answer. He didn't know.

"I think we should go talk to Monte today," she said.

"What the hell for?" Alan asked.

"Why the hell not?" Kathleen countered. "He seems to have a reputation in this town for acting strange out there in the woods and weirding out girls. There might be something to all that."

"I already talked to him," Alan said. "He's a bonafide creep, but I don't believe he's done anything to the girls we're worried about."

Kathleen stood up with a sigh and grabbed Alan's jacket off the hook by the door. She turned, tossing it at him.

"I'm not asking anymore," she said. "Take me to Monte's."

Alan groaned, but knew it wasn't worth arguing with her- she was state police, after all. They always got their way in the end.

Kathleen climbed up in the truck next to Alan and they started down the road toward Pichol Creek. That's when they first spotted Christopher riding along on his bicycle.

"That's the Kendler boy," Alan said, pointing him out. "Dickie's son."

"Another monster hunter," Kathleen said.

Joel chuckled. "None of them are quite as serious about it as Tessie, but I reckon Christopher's the closest. I think his interest is more in keeping her happy than rustling up anything real, though."

Kathleen smiled.

"We should stop and talk to him," she said. "I'd like to meet him and feel him out."

Alan shook his head.

"Nah, I don't think that's a good idea," he said.

"And why not?" she asked. "He was out there the day they found the skeleton. His daddy's tied up right in the middle of the whole thing. Not to mention he's too young to understand the need to lie for anyone. If something was going on that we don't know about, yet, he does. You can count on it."

"That boy's been through enough," Alan said, his voice more firm than before. "Anything he might know, he's better off forgetting, if he's going to have any kind of life at all. History tends to repeat itself if you don't give it another way to go. I don't want to be cutting him down from the trussell in another ten years like his Daddy."

Kathleen sighed. "Yeah, I reckon that's probably about right," she said. "Still, I think if the kid's got something on his conscience it would be good to let him clear it. Kids aren't as dumb as you take them for, Joel. If I've learned anything in my time on this job it's that kids make some of the best witnesses. They just want to help and people underestimate them. They usually understand things a lot bigger than we give them credit for."

Alan brought the car to a stop and turned toward Kathleen with a sigh.

"I don't want you here," he said, bluntly. "I don't think you need to be here and I sure as hell don't feel like I need your help or advice on how to do this investigation. I'm putting up with you because I don't feel like I have a choice in the matter. I will not put up with you messing around, screwing with the heads of the street urchins of Adelaide. I don't admit to having much of a soft spot for anything, but I do for those kids. I want them to grow up with their childhoods as intact as they can be. Are we clear on that?"

Kathleen glared at Alan, sizing him up.

"I think your intentions are good, Sheriff Cline. I just also think you don't know the first thing about kids."

He nodded, rolling his eyes, and put the car back into gear, pulling away.

"I know plenty of things about these kids- and this is non-negotiable."

Chapter Eight

Meanwhile, as Kathleen and Alan were making their way out to talk to Monte, Mama had other plans for our day.

She woke up early and started throwing together a picnic basket full of bologna sandwiches, oatmeal cream pie cookies, vegetable sticks, and potato chips.

I sat at the table with the little ones, slurping the milk from my bowl of Captain Crunch. Nana Carter was in the living room doing her knitting and watching a church program on the television.

"Charlie!" Mama screeched into the back room. "It's time to get up! It's picnic day and we need to stop somewhere and get some Pepsi!"

Charlie groaned from the back room. I could hear the squeaking of the mattress springs as he shifted in the bed in a drag-assing attempt to wake up.

Mom's lips were pursed. Her face was flushing red. I could tell she was getting mad, even if she wasn't saying it outright just yet.

"I told him to get his ass to bed last night," she fumed quietly to herself. "All this mess around here's been more than anyone can handle. If his fucking brother won't worry about himself, nobody else should worry about him, either."

"Mama!" I gasped. "That was the real bad word! You can't say that in front of Devin and Mallory!"

"That's right!" Charlie called from the back room. "You need to calm yourself, Mama! It ain't even ten o'clock yet!"

Mom sucked her teeth. "I know what time it is, Charlie!" she answered. "I also know you well enough to know if I leave you in bed til 10:30, we won't be on the road before two!"

"Where are we going anyway?" I asked. "It's not that far to the park!"

The room filled with an awkward quiet.

"It's Sunday," Mama said, finally.

I didn't understand the significance.

"What difference does that make?" I asked.

Mom took a deep, shaky breath and sighed.

"It's a pretty day for a picnic, Tessie, I'm just trying to get a good spot before the church crowd lets out."

The room got quiet again. I still didn't understand, but with Mama in such a mood I decided I wasn't going to ask any more questions.

The shower started in the back bathroom, causing the water pipes under the kitchen floor to hiss. Mama breathed a sigh of relief.

"He's up at last," she said.

I reached for the cereal to pour a second bowl and she stopped me.

"Tessie!" she said. "Just one! We're going to the park for a picnic lunch soon! You should have got up earlier and ate!"

I grumbled to myself. She was always doing this- making plans without consulting the rest of us. It was usually stupid stuff like picnics in the park or shopping for flowers for the flower bed- Just a lot of things that nobody else really wanted to do, but we had to because she was Mama and we didn't want to make Mama sad.

Looking back, I suppose Mama was just doing her best to try to maintain some sense of normalcy in the chaos that was unfolding all around us.

That's probably why Charlie didn't seem to want to fight her on it as much as he might have in previous times. He was never the kind for picnics in the park, but it seemed like that summer whatever Mama wanted she got. That included dragging us out into the noon-day heat to eat bologna sandwiches under a tree.

By the time we arrived in town at the park, we'd already messed around at home too long and Mama was fuming at the sight of all the cars parked along the gravel surrounding the entrance.

"I knew we'd run into the church crowd," she said with a heavy sigh. "I kept telling y'all to get a move on!"

"Just relax, Mama," Charlie said. "It's going to be just fine. All this means is there will be more kids around for ours to play with."

Mama took a deep breath and forced a sweet smile. "You're right," she said, trying to soothe herself. "It's going to be a good day."

We all piled out of the car, with Mama handing us each something she knew we could manage to carry. I got the picnic basket, which was honestly too heavy for me. My shoulders slumped, fighting against the weight of it, and it knocked against my knees with every step.

She put Mallory, who had to carry nothing, in charge of finding a spot. This, of course, Meant Mallory took off in a dead run down the footpath and around the duck pond, forcing me to wrestle that basket twice as long as what would have been considered humane.

Devin had hauled in the table cloth. He handed it to Mama to spread on the ground and I dropped the picnic basket in the grass as the rest of us waited..

"Don't put the basket in the grass, Tessie!" Mama hollered. "Bugs will get in it!"

I huffed and let out an exhausted growl. Chuckling, Charlie reached down and grabbed the basket, saving me.

With the table cloth spread, Mama motioned for us to bring forth the basket and cooler. As she did, she glanced around us and her expression suddenly changed.

I looked to see what had Mama so upset. All around us, other families were picking up their picnic lunches and moving, giving Charlie dirty glances as they did.

I looked at Charlie.

"What are they mad at you for?" I asked.

He looked at me and shook his head, exhaling a cloud of billowing Marlboro smoke. "They think Joel hurt Ruby," he said. "And they're mad that I don't think it."

It made me angry. My face felt hot with fury and stood up, turning back toward the crowd of people walking away from us.

"You're wrong!" I screamed. "Joel wouldn't hurt nobody!"

"Tessie, stop!" Mama scolded.

But I couldn't.

"You're all stuck-up nosy assholes!"

"TESSIE!" Mama hollered, grabbing me by my arm and dragging me down the path toward the car.

She turned, yelling over her shoulder. "Pack it up, Charlie! We're going!"

"Alright," Charlie yelled back, then changed his tone. Louder. More obvious for passers-by. "We'll find somewhere else to go, y'all! This park's full of trash anyhow!"

Mama stopped dead in her tracks and turned, glaring back at him in furious disbelief.

He looked at her and shrugged.

Another moment passed of the two of them staring at each other, wordless, while the hostile energy of the park misted up all around us.

Then, out of nowhere, Mama started laughing.

"Charlie Westpoole!" She yelled. "What am I going to do with you?"

He motioned toward the table cloth on the ground.

"Come eat these damned sandwiches, for a start," he yelled back, smirking.

All around us, the church people had been caught dead in their tracks. Mouths agape in disbelief, they were shifting their eyes back and forth between us and each other, each waiting for someone else to step in and say something.

Nobody had the guts.

Mama looked down at me, her angry expression softening with her mood.

"Joel didn't do it," I said, leaning my head against her.

"No," she said. "He didn't. You're right.."

She looked around at the crowd. Then, following Charlie's lead, she, too, raised her voice where they could hear her.

"So these motherfuckers can find somewhere else to picnic."

Chapter Nine

When Alan and Kathleen pulled up outside Monte's house, he was sitting on the front porch skinning squirrels into a five-gallon bucket. He looked up at the two of them, then gave Kathleen a long second glance. He flashed her an eerie, ugly grin.

"Who's this, Alan?" he asked.

"Kathleen Quinn," she answered, interrupting before Alan could speak on her behalf. "I'm with the state police. I'm here helping Sheriff Cline get to the bottom of some things and I asked him to bring me out here to meet you."

"Well the pleasure's mine," he said, shifting his pants at the front as he adjusted his position in his chair.

Kathleen turned her face toward Alan in visible disgust as Alan also grimaced, doing his best not to open his mouth and say anything that would ruin the opportunity for Kathleen to sink her teeth in.

"I'm sure you've heard about the girl that's gone missing in town," Kathleen said.

"The Dewey girl!" Monte said, pulling his filthy nails to his teeth and biting. He was doing his best to feign disinterest, but Kathleen could read him like a book. He was getting nervous and she wanted to know why.

"Yes," she said. "Ellen. You know her?"

Monte dropped his hand across his stomach and stared off at the sky, like he was thinking real hard.

"I don't guess I know her outside of just seeing her around up there at the burger joint," he said. "I like to go up there once in a while. I like them big hot dogs they got. I'll get one of them and a coke for supper if I get a little extra cash."

Kathleen smiled and nodded.

"But you know her name?" she said. "So you must have taken some kind of an interest in her."

Monte stood up and shifted his weight on his feet. He was getting more flustered as the questions kept coming.

"Well her name's been in the paper!" he said. "Plus Adelaide ain't big. Everyone knows everybody's names."

Kathleen didn't stand down. "Did you get yourself one of those dogs on the night she disappeared? If we check that camera, am I going to see your truck?"

"Yes!" Monte said, not hesitating. "I got one that night."

"About what time?" Alan asked, interrupting.

Kathleen turned toward Alan, shooting him an icy stare. She wasn't used to being interrupted.

He rolled his eyes back at her. He wasn't used to playing second fiddle.

"I don't recall," Monte said. "It was past dark, though. I don't like going into town during the daytime much. I don't like how people act around me. After dark, nobody gives me much mind."

"Was it around closing?" Kathleen asked. "It's been getting dark real late lately, so it must have been."

Monte scrunched his nose. His eyes became dark and wicked. He was no longer looking at Kathleen with any kind of adoration. That had been replaced with fury.

"If what you want to know is whether or not I went up there and kidnapped Ellen Dewey, then you need to just come right out and ask that, Ma'am."

Kathleen smiled.

"Did you, Monte? Did you go up there and kidnap Ellen Dewey? Did you kill her? Is she laying out here in these woods somewhere?"

Monte raised his chin, staring down his nose in indignation. He took a slow sidestep to the top of the porch stairs and carefully, slowly eased his way down. As he did, he approached Kathleen.

Alan stepped back, shielding his right hip behind the car. On his hip, his hand rested on the back strap of his gun, preparing to draw if needed.

"You ain't gotta shoot me, Cline," Monte said, monotone, never gazing over in Alan's direction. "I aint gonna hurt her."

"Well what are you going to do?" Kathleen asked, raising her own chin now- squaring up on Monte to show she was not intimidated.

He sneered, staring down at her face, then lowering his gaze to her breasts.

"Back it up, Monte," Alan called.

Kathleen took a half step back, zipping her jacket all the way up.

Seeing this, Monte started to laugh.

"Ellen might be out in these woods," he said, shrugging. "Or she might not be. You asked whether I went up there with intent to take her, the answer's no. I was hungry. I wanted a hot dog. That ain't no crime."

"But did you take her?" Alan asked. His voice had grown more stern. "Cut the bullshit, Monte, and tell us what happened."

Monte stepped back, walking slowly backward toward his porch. He turned his attention to Alan now, smiling.

"From what I hear, y'all don't even know that she's dead," he laughed. "So you got a lot of nerve coming out here accusing me of anything. Good luck on your investigation. I've got nothing I can say that will be of any help to y'all. I just want you to quit coming out here. You're harassing me now."

Alan looked toward Kathleen. She returned his glance with a nod.

"Then I guess we gotta go, Alan," she said. "But first- I can't help but notice there's a guitar laying under your porch, Monte."

She pointed to an opening where the old wooden lattice had rotted away, opening a gap in the porch skirting.

"Odd place for it," she said. "Do you play?"

"There's all kinds of junk out here," he said. "Used to have an old dog that slept under the porch there. He's what knocked away all that lattice wood. He would find shit and drag it under there. I don't pay nothin' no mind."

"Shame," she said. "Looks like it could have been a pretty guitar at one point. Real pretty strap on it. What's that embroidery on it? Is it tiger lilies?"

Montle stepped back off his porch, taking a firm, angry step toward Kathleen.

"I said I'm done talking!" He hollered. "It's time for you folks to go."

Chapter Ten

The sun was low and heavy in the sky, casting long shadows that stretched across the yard like dark fingers as Alan as he arrived the following evening back at Monte's rundown property. Monte's place always gave Alan an uneasy feeling, like walking into a spider's web and not knowing where the spider was. The trees swayed gently with the wind, their whispers seeming to carry secrets too dark for daylight.

The yard, littered with what decades' worth of hoarding brought, seemed desolate- more so now with the conspicuous absence of that old guitar that had caught Kathleen's eye the day before.

Ruby's for sure, Alan thought, a knot forming in the pit of his stomach. He had hoped to talk to Monte about it and maybe clear up a few nagging doubts, but the man also was nowhere to be found.

As Alan left the property and came to a stop at the crossroads, a dust cloud heralded the arrival of a Charlie's pick up, meeting Alan at the intersection.

Though still angry with Alan, Charlie was curious what he was doing at Monte's. As the two cars sat idling at the four-way, Charlie rolled his window down and motioned for Alan to pull off for a chat, his expression a mix of concern and curiosity.

When the two had parked, Alan got out of his car and approached Charlie, leaning against the bed of his truck.

"Evenin', Alan," Charlie greeted, stepping out of his truck, his boots crunching on the gravel. "Lookin' for Monte?"

"Yeah," Alan replied, wiping the sweat from his brow. "Seems like he's out, though. Didn't happen to cross paths with him anywhere, did ya? Or see an old guitar tossed off somewhere?"

Charlie's eyes narrowed, the gears in his head visibly turning. "Guitar? Ruby's, maybe?"

Alan kept his face neutral. "Might be. Why? You know something about it?"

Instead of answering, Charlie exhaled, long and slow, his gaze shifting to the thickening shadows. "You know you've got the wrong man, Alan. It can't be Joel. It just can't."

"And why do you think that?" Alan asked, raising an eyebrow, interested in Charlie's change of demeanor.

Charlie looked like he'd aged years in seconds. "She came by the house that night– Ruby did. All frantic-like, with Monte in tow, babbling about needing to talk to Joel- about bein' pregnant."

"Pregnant?" Alan asked, raising an eyebrow. Until that moment, Charlie had pretended not to know that Ruby was carrying.

"Yeah," Charlie's voice was heavy with regret. "But I knew. I knew deep down in my bones that the baby wasn't Joel's. Ruby was... she was lost, tryin' to anchor herself to anything, anyone.- and Joel would have let her anchor up to him, even knowing he wasn't the father. He'd have stepped up and stuck his foot right in it."

"So, what did you do, Charlie?" Alan asked, suddenly more worried than he'd anticipated at the beginning of the conversation.

Charlie's eyes, filled with a sorrow that comes from carrying' a burdensome secret for too long, met Alan's.

"I gave her money. Five thousand dollars. It was all I had squirreled away. Told her to leave and never come back."

The confession hung in the air between them, heavy and pungent like the scent before a rainstorm.

Alan's mind raced. Ruby, pregnant and scared, had been turned away by the one family she might have been counting on years ahead of her grim finale This chapter of her story silenced until now.

"And Joel?" Alan finally asked, his voice hoarse.

Charlie leaned against his truck, arms crossed over his chest as if hugging himself, maybe seeking some comfort or maybe just trying to hold himself together. His eyes didn't meet Alan's anymore.

Instead, they were lost somewhere in the growing dusk, caught in the memories of a time he wished he could forget.

"Ruby was... a firecracker, y'know?" Charlie began, his voice barely more than a murmur. "Full of life, but not the steady kind. More like a twister. She'd pull you in, and before you knew it, you'd be spinnin' so fast, you couldn't tell up from down."

He took a long drag of his cigarette, then continued right along in the re-telling.

"She wasn't good for Joel, Alan. My brother's got an ego as big as these mountains, but he's fragile, in a way. He gets fixated on things and can't let 'em go. He was obsessed with the idea of saving Ruby from herself–from her life. But you can't save someone who don't wanna be saved, can you?"

Charlie's eyes were hauntingly hollow, the weight of his regret settling in them like sediment.

"Joel didn't see, or maybe didn't wanna see, the storms inside her. Ruby partied hard, got mixed up with all sorts, took things she shouldn't. I was scared- real scared- that she'd drag Joel down with her. He'd marry her, tryin' to do right by her and the baby, not realizing he was tying himself to a runaway stem engine headed straight for Hell."

Charlie pushed himself off his truck to the gravel road and started pacing, restless like a caged animal.

"And that night, she shows up, saying she's carrying Joel's baby, which I knew could not be true. Me and him talk. I'm not an idiot. I looked into her eyes, Alan, and I saw it – the chaos, the desperation. It wasn't just about the baby; it was her last grasp at having someone to tie her down and keep her steady. And I couldn't let that someone be my baby brother."

He stopped and turned to Alan, a desperate plea in his eyes. "I had to protect him, you know? From her and from the heartbreak and mayhem she'd bring. So, I gave her the money thinking she'd go start fresh in Nashville and meet someone else and forget about him just like we all thought she actually did. I never...," his voice broke, "I never thought we'd end up here."

The evening cicadas began their chorus as an eerie backdrop to a tale of misguided decisions and lost lives. Alan could see it all now - the fear for a brother's future and the frantic hope that money could solve a problem too deep-rooted to untangle. He saw the tragedy that unfolded from choices made with trembling hands and a quaking heart.

"Did you give her cash?" Alan asked, now recognizing that robbery had suddenly entered the scene as a possible motive.

Charlie nodded.

"I did," he said, his voice breaking from the same realization.

And just like that- as the first stars pricked the night sky, a story of love, protection, and profound regret had found its voice in the hush of fading Adelaide summer light.

Chapter Eleven

The memory of the day Chris Kendler went missing is as vivid as the bright summer sun that hung in the sky, burnin' up the horizon and promisin' a break from the dark clouds we'd been livin' under.

Brittany and I had finally been allowed to hang out together and we were like two wild birds released from a cage, peddling down the streets of Adelaide on our bikes like we had not one care in the world.

It was the first time in weeks we really felt like the children we actually were. I was just a sprout, all arms and legs and fiery red hair I hadn't yet learned to tame. And Brittany- that girl was the other half of my soul, wild and free, laughin' with her whole body. Her folks had been keeping her locked up tight. They said it was too dangerous to be gallivantin' about with a murderer still breathing our air. But- that day, they'd loosened their grip just enough for us to slip out together, two peas burstin' from the same pod.

We were riding our bikes down the old town roads, the dusty trails kicking up behind us. Our laughter was bubbling in the air, catching the wind and echoing back like it didn't want to leave us just yet. And then, there it was, outta place in a day so filled with life- Charlie's beat-up truck, parked outside the jail like a bad omen.

We skidded to a halt, our bikes rattling something fierce, and our eyes wide as saucers. There was a tension between us, buzzin' like electricity, settling heavy in our young bones. But then the jailhouse door creaked open, and out stepped Charlie, looking like the weight of the world had just been lifted off his broad shoulders-and there, right next to him, was Joel. My heart near about catapulted from my chest.

"Joel!" I couldn't help the way my voice cracked, shattering the heavy air as I ran toward him, my legs pumping faster than I thought they could go.

He was smiling, but his eyes were telling a different story. He was twice as tired as he'd ever been. "Tessie," he said, his voice like a song I'd thought I'd forgotten. "You get on home now. We're gonna have ourselves a celebration, you hear?"

The world came rushing back. The colors were brighter and the sounds louder. I grabbed Brittany's hand, our fingers interlocking, and we flew back to our bikes to make our way out to the house- but first, we had someone to tell.

Christopher had to know. He'd been wearing his worry for Joel like a heavy coat in July, wrinkling his brows up every time someone mentioned the man's name.

But when we got to his place, what we found knocked the air right out of us. His rickety old bike was just lying there in the middle of the road, lookin' lost and lonesome and there was no sign of Chris, himself.

"Christopher!" Brittany's voice was a thin screech, like the sound of a kettle forgotten on the stove. We called for him, our voices meldin' together in a chorus of panic, but there was no answer save for the mournful whistle of the wind through the trees.

Dread settled in my gut, heavy and cold, making my insides churn. This wasn't right. Christopher wouldn't just leave his bike-not like that. He treated that thing like it was made of gold, always polishing it even though rust was winning the war.

We searched in the thickets, down by the creek, and up by the holler where we'd once found a bird's nest resting low in an old oak. But it was like the earth had just swallowed him whole.

The joy of Joel's release curdled fast in our hearts, replaced by a fear sharp as a knife's edge. Our little world, it seemed, was never gonna be free of shadows, no matter how bright the sun shone down on us.

As we stood there, our hands still clutched tight, I remember thinking that life was this messy, tangling bramble. You'd free yourself from one snag, only to get caught up in another. I didn't know then, couldn't know, the way the briars would keep twistin' and turnin', making us part of a story that was bigger and darker than the secrets whispered in the dead of night.

But that day, with Christopher's bike cast aside and him nowhere to be found, I felt it. Something was coming, creeping up slow and determined like ivy climbing a wall.

Chapter Twelve

In the tapestry of time, there's always that one thread- that one day that, when pulled, unravels the peace of a community, leaving nothing but frayed ends and hearts in its wake. In our sleepy corner of Virginia, that day came with a sky full of promises, dawn yawnin' lazy and golden over the ridge, not hinting at all at the darkness that was about to sink its teeth in on us.

It was a day that would etch itself into the annals of our history, not gentle-like, with the soft whisper of a lover's promise, but with the violent urgency of lightning' striking' dry timber. Some folks around town would come to call it "The Whispering Woe," because that's what it did — whispered slowly a woeful tale so grim it felt like the sun wouldn't ever find Adelaide whole again.

My world was only as big as the holler and no bigger, but even I could feel it- that electric charge of something' coming, stirring the air, making the hairs on the back of my neck stand to attention. It was the kind of day where the cicadas sang a bit too loud, the air hung a bit too heavy, and the folks whispered a bit too quiet. As fate, with her cruel humor, would have it, Brittany and me were searching high and low for Christopher at the same time Kathleen was about to step into a fiery twist in Ellen's case.

Nobody knew it yet- and especially not Kathleen. Her thoughts were tangled up in the cold case files spread across her desk and the phantom faces of the lost and the silent begging her for answers. She was drowning in the 'what-ifs' and 'whys,' as her coffee was growing cold next to the stack of reports echoing Ruby's unsung songs- a melody of a life stopped short and a riddle wrapped in the deep green mystery of Pichol Creek.

Poor Alan, bless his heart, he was out there pacing the dusty aisles of Ferguson's Five-and-Dime, listening to old Mrs. Henderson's detailed account of the neighborhood kids who'd taken to a five-finger discount before running off with their pockets heavy on candy bars they didn't pay no mind to payin' for. His radio crackled with the mundane: the small thieveries and even smaller disputes. He was a world away from the storm that was brewing under the deceiving calm, occupied with the ledger of small town life.

They were both oblivious to the fact that Chris's mama was frantically turning every rock in Adelaide upside down, her sense of calm getting swallowed up by the same woods that kept our darkest secrets. It's a peculiar thing how life makes you juggle hope and despair, often at the same time-often in the same heart.

"The Whispering Woe" didn't just see the sun travel across the sky. It saw hope flicker and wane in the eyes of our townsfolk. It was the day when childhoods were cut short and the lines between the past and the present, between memories and nightmares, got blurred beyond recognition. It was when Adelaide lost a piece of its innocence- the kind you can't never find nor put back, no matter how you try.

It was Kathleen who got the news whilst she

was perched like a vigilant hawk in the sheriff's office.

Old crazy Elma Jacobs was the harbinger. Her hair white as the dogwood blossoms come April was usually pinned back neat, but that day it was flyin' every which way.

Elma lived in a cramped, musty apartment above Cassidy's old hardware store. That little space was a sanctuary for her and her feline army — all six of 'em, last I'd counted, perched in the front windows looking down over Main Street like lions surveying the Sahara.

I'd asked her their names once, but they were all named after a bunch of boring old poets, so I'd forgotten the names almost as quick as I'd learned them.

What really set Elma apart wasn't just the company she kept, but also her escapades into the woods. She'd venture under the canopy of oaks and pines at the oddest hours, wild and free like the spirit she was. In her hands, she'd clutch an old wicker basket, frayed from years of use, and she'd come back with it overflowing with what she claimed was wild catnip, but Charlie always said that under that top layer of sprigs, there was a different kind of plucked plant- one with leaves- and she wasn't out there collecting it for no kitty cats.

Folks in town would watch from behind screen doors and curtains as she traipsed down Main Street with her worn-out boots muddy and a triumphant sparkle in those keen, nut-brown eyes. She'd swear up and down about the "healing properties" of her gatherings, how they'd soothe her cats' nerves and keep them youthful.

Some folks chuckled, others shook their heads, but in her heart, Elma held an unshakable belief in the wonders she'd plucked from the earth's bosom.

She was a solitary figure, not the kind you'd see at Sunday service or sipping sweet tea at community gatherings. No- Elma marched to the beat of her own drum, humming a tune all her own. And while her ways might've been the talk of the town, there was something about her untamed nature- a quiet defiance of the mundane- that you couldn't help but admire. She was a wildflower steadfast amidst conforming fields of corny stalks.

And if there was one thing about Elma that everyone in Adelaide agreed on, it was this: You could count on her. Her beliefs might be shaky, but she believed them wholeheartedly and she was not one to ever tell a lie.

She came into the sheriff's office that morning panting and her cheeks flushed and her eyes wide as saucers. Everyone that was there said the poor thing looked like she'd seen a ghost- or worse.

She went off rattling a mile a minute 'bout seeing Monte prancing around the woods naked and bloody, actin' a fool and doing things to himself that'd make even a seasoned lady like herself blush.

She said there was a darkness in his eyes- like the devil himself was dancing behind them.

Kathleen, she just sat there quiet, absorbing Elma's words like the thirsty earth soaks up rain after a drought. As the gears went clicking into place in her mind, she decided she'd be the one to confront Monte. She was set to corner him with his own sins, believing in her heart of hearts that she could make him confess to Ruby's murder and maybe, just maybe, find out what happened to sweet Ellen too.

When she got to Monte's though, she didn't find him. He and his truck were long gone- and his house was up in blazes, roaring out, laughing in the face of justice as Kathleen stood, mouth agape, knowing she'd just missed him- and he'd taken hauled off with every secret she needed to unravel if she was ever going to find Ellen Dewey alive.

And it was right then and there- under the harsh glow of that inferno- the whispering woe began to murmur.

Chapter Thirteen

The dawn that broke over Adelaide the next morning was laden with a heaviness that could darn near crush a man's spirit. It felt like a sack of wet cotton had been laid across the town, seeping deep into our bones. Though the sun was doing its damndest to shine, it could do nothing to lighten the hearts of those who loved little Chris Kendler.

My favorite boy had up and disappeared, as if, just like Monte's house, he'd turned to smoke and been whisked away by the breeze.

Alan, with more years and troubles under his belt than most, had a look about him I'd neer seen before. His eyes, usually as soft as clean bed sheets, hardened into stones and his jaw clenched up tighter than a steel trap. Kathleen managed to keep her calm exterior, but beneath it, you could feel the fierce current of her thoughts, racing and churning like a river beneath a layer of winter ice.

A shiver ran down Adelaide's spine, leaving folks whispering and throwing glances over their shoulders, clutching their young'uns just a little bit closer.

Adversity, though, has a funny way of making a community ball up its fists and square its shoulders, ready to throw punches at the dark- and Adelaide came armed with nothing but stubbornness and grit.

Alan and Kathleen weren't ones to dilly-dally and this was especially true when it came to a child.

Alerts were flying out faster than bats at dusk, crackling over radios and painting the airwaves with descriptions of Chris. The whole town was praying' that someone-anyone-had caught a glimpse of the boy.

"Keep your eyes peeled," Alan's voice would boom, a hidden layer of urgency turning his words sharp.

At the same time, amidst the flurry for Chris, they also cast a net wide and far for any trace of Monte and his beat-up red truck. "We ain't pointin' fingers or jumping' to conclusions," Alan would say, voice steady as a rock. "But it's crucial we find Monte for other matters and to rule him out as having anything to do with the Kendler boy's disappearance."

Now, folks in Adelaide ain't fools. They'd seen enough trouble to know that when scandal starts singing, it doesn't sing solo.

Alan kept on trying to keep the gossip to a minimum, though. He told the people what they needed to hear, but when the cameras were off and he wasn't needing to try to keep up any kind of media charade, you could see it – the doubt, the worry, and that thin thread of fear that maybe all these events really were woven from the same dark cloth.

Adelaide held its breath, the air heavy as a preacher's pause, waitin' to see what hand fate was gonna deal.

Hearts reached out in silent prayer and hope, wishing for Chris's safe return and for answers to unfold.

But that's when the vultures descended.

News vans from near and far swarmed in, brandishing microphones and cameras like weapons in a war for the most sensational angle. Alan found himself in the eye of the storm, surrounded by a sea of pushy reporters, each one hungrier than the last for a juicy bit of drama.

"What about Ruby? Any leads on her murderer?" one would demand.

"And Ellen? Is there a connection to Chris Kendler's disappearance?" another would pipe up, their questions weaving' a web of insinuation and suspicion.

"What can you tell us about Monte? Is he a suspect in all this? What's being done to find him?" The questions came hard and fast, relentless in their pursuit of a salacious story.

Amidst the chaos, one slick reporter threw out a curveball. "Sheriff Cline," he drawled, all eyes suddenly on him, "This situation-it's gotta remind you of what happened at your last post, right? That was a rough patch, wasn't it?"

The crowd fell silent. The air was tense as a drawn bowstring. Alan's jaw clenched, his eyes hardening to chips of flint. He didn't answer, just shot a look that could curdle milk. Whatever happened in Alan's past stayed buried, but the rumors took flight like crows from an old beat down scarecrow.

Then, a soft-spoken reporter with eyes wide and innocent, dropped another bombshell that sucked the air right out of the room..

"We've heard rumors," she began, her voice trembling' like she was walking' on holy ground. "Is there any truth in the story that Chris Kendler's father, Dickie, took his own life earlier this summer? He was brought in for questioning about Ruby, only shortly before that, wasn't he?"

Alan went white as a ghost, his face was a mask of shock and fury. Dickie Kendler's pain was supposed to be a private sorrow, not fodder for the evening news.

The pressure in that moment was like a powder keg ready to blow.

The tragedy of Adelaide was morphing into a national spectacle with all our rawest wounds laid bare for the world to see.

For us,this wasn't just a news story. This was our lives, bleeding out in front of a captive audience.

This was no longer just Adelaide's burden to bear. It had become the country's latest obsession. Our tragedy was being served up for supper on the evening news.

Chapter Fourteen

When you're a little one, the world's a simple place, or so it seems. Good folks, bad folks, and the monsters that lurk in the dark corners of your world are all separated into clearly outlined categories.

But what nobody tells you is that, sometimes, the worst monsters don't hide under your bed. Sometimes they sit right at your dinner table, passing you the mashed potatoes.

I learned that lesson earlier than most and it near about broke me. But minds, especially young ones, have a way of mending what's shattered.

Mine did so by clinging to other monsters- the kind you find in dusty old library books and whispered stories by firelight.

The night Mama took a stand against Daddy, the night she had no choice but to end his reign of terror to save her own life and mine- that was the night something inside little Tessie splintered. I reckon it was my belief in the simple nature of good and evil-the trust that those who're meant to love you won't turn into something fearsome and unrecognizable.

After that, the world wasn't the same. It was as if I woke up and all the colors had bled dry.

So, I turned to other tales where the monsters weren't Daddy's eyes flashing in the dim light, or the bruises that Mama tried to hide. I buried myself in stories of creatures like the Nereids, beautiful but terrible, demanding' sacrifices of lovely maidens out of pure envy. They dwelt in places like Pichol Creek.

These monsters.. they were safer, see? They weren't supposed to be protecting you or loving you. They didn't break your heart by becoming something other than what they always were. They were just monsters, plain and simple. Somehow, that made my world a bit more bearable, giving me a way to make sense of things that no child should ever have to understand.

My obsession didn't spring from family lore or ancestral tales. It was born in the quiet aisles of our local library, where I'd lose myself in the labyrinth of legends nestled within crinkled pages. Books upon books, I devoured them, each story a seed sown in the fertile soil of my imagination. Among those seeds, the Nereids took root. They were water nymphs of captivating beauty, but vicious jealousy and I purported them as dwellers of our very own Pichol Creek.

When Chris went missing, my mind didn't dart to the evils men do. It raced straight to the shadowed waters and the myths I'd nestled close to my heart. Those Nereids had taken him, I reckoned, aiming to use him to snatch his beautiful mama. It was a wild theory, but fear skews your world in ways you never thought possible.

So, under a sky sprinkled with stars like scattered grains of sugar, I gathered Brittany, Erik, and Josh at the edge of the woods, unveiling my plan to stake out Pichol Creek bridge. I was ablaze with purpose, but my friends...they didn't share the flame.

They stood there in a huddle of skepticism against my wild conviction, as I laid it all out. Brittany, bless her, she'd always been the ground to my flight. She heard me out, though, despite her expression souring like she'd bitten a lemon.

"Tessie," she interrupted, her voice a no-nonsense kind of stern. "Nereids? Really? You know this ain't one of your storybooks, right? Chris was taken by someone real, not...not some creek mermaid."

I kept right on. "But the Nereids, they're jealous creatures, they want Debbie, and—"

"Tessie." Her word was a stop sign, hand on hip, the other outstretched like she was trying' to physically corral my thoughts. "There ain't no Nereids. No mandrake roots, no werewolves, no tailypos...and no Santa Claus, while we're at it. What happened to Ruby, to Ellen, now Chris... it's real-life scary, not make-believe."

Her words settled heavy, like stones in the pit of my stomach. Around us, Erik and Josh shuffled awkwardly, eyes rooted to the ground as if it held answers. The woods were silent. Complicit.

We argued next. Under the trees that had heard countless secrets, our words were fireflies, darting sharp and angry in the dark, each "realistic" retort from Brittany a pinprick to the world we'd built together in those woods.

When all was said and done, though, we were just four kids in the woods, straddling the line between the world we wanted and the one we were in.

The silence hung between us like a fog, each of us marooned in our own uncertainties. My eyes flickered to Josh and Erik, searching or an ally. Surely, they could see? The world was vast, brimming with unfathomable wonders and terrors alike. Why not Nereids?

Josh scratched the back of his neck, his gaze shifting uneasily. "Tessie," he started, voice low, "I reckon we've all had a great time chasing monsters and pretending we're in one of your stories, but this ain't the same. This is real, like what happened to Ruby and Ellen. We can't just pretend it's somethin' out of a book. It ain't fun when it's real...when real people get hurt."

His words, though gentle, felt like a door closing. I wanted to rage and scream that it wasn't just pretend-that sometimes the world really was as strange and terrible as the books said. The plea died in my throat, though, strangled by the weight of fear.

I didn't want to argue anymore. I didn't want them to convince me out of my beliefs because giving up what I believed would mean facing another harsh reality- and I was sick as hell of doing that.

I looked over at Erik, who always brought up the rear on our adventures. He seemed to always be more a shadow than a participant, so I didn't carry much hope he'd take my side.

He stepped forward, though, with a quiet kind of resolve that tugged at my heart.

"I don't reckon I believe in Nereids or any of those things, Tessie," he said, his voice steady, "But you believe. And that's good enough for me. You shouldn't have to face this alone. I'll go with you."

I felt a quiver in my lip and a stinging in my eyes. It wasn't the grand speech of a knight vowing to slay dragons, but to my young, frightened heart, it was a lifeline. Brittany and Josh, their faces tight, turned away then, receding back toward the safety of what was known and seen- what was human. As they faded into the comforting embrace of skepticism, Erik stayed there by me- a quiet sentinel in my world of monsters and myths.

"Thank you," I whispered, the words barely disturbing the heavy air around us.

Erik shrugged, a small smile warming his features. "We all got our monsters, Tess. Real or not, doesn't matter. What matters is we don't let 'em beat us, right?"

Right, I thought. No matter how real the monsters were, we couldn't let them win. With Erik by my side, I felt a tiny bit stronger and a whole lot less alone.

"Together, we'll stake out Pichol Creek bridge, and wait for that monster," I said. "But not tonight. Mama's gonna be mad if I don't get on home soon."

Erik nodded. "We'll go when you're ready," he said. Because that's what you do for friends. You stand with them, whether you're facing down a figment or a fear-a myth or a murderer.

Chapter Fifteen

It's a peculiar thing, watching' the world you thought you knew turn upside down and inside out on a flickering TV screen. There, in our cramped living room, with the wallpaper peelin' just a bit at the corners and the air heavy with the scent of Momma's beef stew simmering away, it seemed like any other evening. But it wasn't. The images on the television were proof enough of that. The news had been buzzing like an angry hornet ever since the reporters descended on Adelaide, stirring up more trouble than a twister in June.

Momma and I were sitting on our old couch with the stuffing coming out in places. Our eyes were fixed on the screen. She had her hand on her belly, gentle-like, as if to shield the baby from the world's madness.

And there he was-Sheriff Alan Cline, lookin' like a deer caught in headlights. His usual composed demeanor was crumbling as the reporters swarmed him like vultures on a fresh carcass. They were jabbering about something from his past-something scandalous from when he was sheriff over in Sanders.

"Momma, what's this all about?" I asked, squinting at the screen, tryin' to make sense of the commotion.

"Hush, Tessie," she said, her eyes never leaving the glowing box. "Let's just listen."

And listen we did. Alan's voice, usually so sure

and comforting, broke through the craziness. He looked straight into the camera, deciding then and there, it seemed, to bare his soul for all the world to see.

"Alright, enough!" he practically hollered, rubbing his forehead as if trying to ward off a mighty headache.

"Yes, I made a mistake, a judgment in error. It was a long time ago," he continued, his voice softening but every word clear as crystal. "I became involved with a woman. She...she was the mother of a suspect in a murder case I was investigating."

The reporters erupted, their voices climbing over one another, but Alan held up his hand, demanding silence. "The suspect was cleared, found innocent," he added quickly. "Folks started talkin', saying my relationship had clouded my judgment-that I'd let things slide. It wasn't true, but the damage was done. I left Sanders, came here to start fresh. Thought I'd left all that behind."

Momma let out a long sigh, shaking her head. "Life has a way of following you," she murmured, more to herself than me.

I frowned, feeling a sting of pity for the man. "But he's a good sheriff, ain't he, Momma?"

"The best we've had, Tessie," she affirmed, patting my hand. "But folks like to tear down what they don't understand and build stories outta half-truths and whispers."

We sat in silence as the reporters on screen prattled on, speculating on what this revelation meant for the cases at hand. Ruby, Ellen, Chris- they were all intertwined in this mess and now Alan's past was tangled up in it, too.

It was a lot for a young mind to take in. I couldn't make sense of all these secrets spillin' out. It got me thinking about monsters again- the real ones that wore human faces and carried their darkness inside them, quiet and secret. I shivered, leaning into Mama's warmth.

"Monsters ain't just in stories, are they, Momma?" I whispered, already knowing' the answer.

"No, baby," she whispered back, pullin' me close. "But remember, there's good in this world, too. More good than bad, I reckon."

I nodded, wanting so bad to believe her. But with the TV casting' shadows across the room, and the night pressing in close, it was hard to see the good through the gathering dark.

Still, I held on tight to Mama's words, like they were a lifeline in a storm. If anyone knew about fighting monsters and finding the light, it was her. I figured, if she could still believe, then maybe I could, too.

The news segment shifted back to Alan and it looked like the vultures weren't done picking at him yet.

Another reporter, a sharp-faced woman with

a voice like a saw cutting through pine, stepped forward, mic in hand.

"Sheriff Cline," she called out. "Given your past indiscretions, is there anything that might be clouding your judgment in this case?"

Mama tensed beside me, her fingers digging slightly into my shoulder. The room felt smaller all of a sudden, the air thicker. On screen, Alan's jaw worked like he was chewing on the question, figuring the taste of it.

"Nothin's cloudin' my judgment," he finally said, his voice steady as a summer breeze. "I solved the murder case back in Sanders, despite all the talk, and I'll solve this one, too. My personal life has no bearing on my ability to serve and protect this community."

The reporter tried to push, her words poking and prodding like she was trying to get him to trip up and spill something he didn't mean to, but Alan was stone- all sharp edges and solid surface.

"We're doing everything in our power to find Chris and get to the bottom of what happened to Ruby and Ellen," he continued, his gaze as sincere as a preacher. "We're followin' every lead, turning over every stone and we won't rest until we have answers."

I felt a squeeze in my chest, thinking about Chris out there somewhere, maybe alone and scared.

Or like Ruby- gone forever.

It was a heavy load of sorrow, settling deep in my bones.

"He's doing his best, ain't he, Mama?" I asked, searching her face for reassurance.

She nodded slowly, her eyes clouded with thoughts she didn't speak aloud. "Yes, baby, he is. Sometimes a person's best is all they have to give."

We watched in silence as the screen filled with images of the town's folks, their faces drawn and worried. The reporters were all throwing out speculation like candy at a parade and asking people on the streets of Adelaide to do the same. It was all just noise, though- a buzzing that filled the town, echoing the fear that clung to the walls of all our homes.

I snuggled closer to Mama, letting her presence be a comfort in the midst of chaos. She kissed the top of my head, and for a moment- just a small one- it felt like it used to before monsters became more than just tales whispered in the dark.

The TV kept chattering, but I let my mind drift, aw

Chapter Sixteen

That evening, the sky a murky soup of twilight, I was on the phone with Erik- our words hushed as if the walls had ears.

"Erik, we gotta do this," I whispered, clutching the receiver so tight my knuckles ached. "If the nereids have Chris, he don't have long! If you can't come with me, I can go by myself, though."

There was a pause, the kind heavy with thought, before he replied. "Tess, I don't know about mermaids or any of that stuff, but I know you shouldn't go alone."

A warmth spread through my chest-gratitude for having a friend brave enough to wade through crazy waters with me.

"We should write notes, Erik," I proposed, a lump forming in my throat. "We gotta write letters to our moms, just in case we don't come back."

His silence was answer enough, agreement and fear mingled tight.

So, as I waited for Erik to sneak out of his home and head my way, I set to it, penning down what I knew might be my last recorded words. My hand trembled as I scribbled, the pen skittering across the paper.

Dear Mama,

I know you'll be mad, and I know you might not understand, but I've gone to help Chris. There's something in the creek, Mama. It's something dark and slippery and hateful and when I finally stop it, Chris and Ellen can come home. I can't just let it keep doing this. I have to help my friend.

I love you more than all the stars in the sky and to the moon and back. And I'm sorry for this and all the times I wasn't a good kid.

Please remember that, always.

– Tessie

I tucked the note under my pillow and snuck out of the house, then ran to the edge of the woods to meet Erik.

When he arrived, we planned with the precision of generals how we'd defeat the nereids. Our backpacks were packed with flashlights, snacks, and, absurd as it sounded, a mirror — I'd read Nereids were vain and a reflection could distract them.

There was a haunting echo in the stillness of the woods as we looked out toward the creek.

"You ready?" Erik asked, his voice quivering just a touch.

"As I'll ever be," I admitted. My heart was pounding like a drumbeat in my chest.

We moved through the night, our steps whispering against the earth. The bridge loomed ahead- the creek's song singing a melody beneath it.

Settling in, we huddled close for warmth as the chill of the night seeped into our bones. Hours ticked by, each feeling like a lifetime. Our eyes searched the waters, the banks, and the shadows between the trees until we both fell asleep.

As dawn painted the sky in strokes of pink and gold, we woke and found ourselves empty-handed. No nereids graced us with their terror, no Chris stumbled from the woods, and no answers revealed themselves in the gurgling waters of Pichol Creek.

Defeated, we trudged back toward our bikes with the weight of the world heavy on our young shoulders.

Upon return, the relief in Mama's eyes was a stab to my guilty heart. The note, I saw, lay untouched on my bed. Erik got an earful from his mom over the phone, though. Her voice echoed through the receiver as a shrill punctuation to our failure.

In the light of day, with the normalcy of life buzzing around us, our adventure seemed foolish.

Monsters were real, though. I knew that much. Whether they had scales and tails or flesh and blood like you and me, they were out there.

And maybe, just maybe, we were lucky we hadn't found them.

Chapter Seventeen

Kathleen had always been the kind to hold her worries close, like cards in a high-stakes game of poker, but after the news broadcast that ruffled the feathers of our small town, those worries spilled over.

I wasn't there to see it, but the tension that had been brewing between her and Alan was common knowledge, almost as palpable as the summer humidity.

In the sanctuary of the sheriff's office, where the law was supposed to find solace, Kathleen cornered Alan.

"Alan, we need to talk," she started, not a request, but a demand-her voice taut as a wire.

Alan, a man who wore his authority like a second skin, looked up, weary. His desk was a fortress of paperwork-the clutter a testament to the storm he was navigating.

"Kathleen, if this is about the news—"

"It is about the news, Alan, and it's about Joel, and Chris, and everything that's been happening. I watched you out there, cornered like a rattlesnake ready to strike. What was all that about Sanders?" Her words were rapid-fire, sharpened to a point.

Alan's sigh was a heavy thing, filled with the ghosts of past mistakes. "Kathleen, that was a long time ago. It was just a bunch of bullshit that held no water."

"Accusations don't come from thin air, Alan," she countered, eyes flashing. "Why is everyone so sure you messed that case up if you really did solve it?"

Alan's silence spoke volumes, his jaw setting. "It was a complicated time. Her son was in trouble- deep trouble- and she and I just happened. The boy was cleared and the real perpetrator found but not before everyone got their fill of weaving up tales about it. You know how these things go!"

"But there was doubt, wasn't there?" Kathleen pressed, relentless. "Doubt that you were thinking straight, so now, I've gotta ask.. with Joel..."

Alan's chair scraped back as he scooted and stood.. "You think I'd let personal history repeat itself? You think I'd put anyone else's life in jeopardy like that?"

"Not intentionally, no," Kathleen conceded, her voice softer now, but no less firm. "But Alan, you've got a soft spot for that family. Can you honestly tell me that doesn't cloud your judgment, even a little?"

The air between them was electric, charged with unsaid words and fears unvoiced.

"That family's been through enough," Alan admitted, his voice gravelly with emotion. "I do have a soft spot for them, I won't deny it. And Joel's a good man. He's a little hotheaded, sure, but he's not the one that killed Ruby. I'm sure of that and you're just going to have to believe me."

Kathleen looked at him, skeptical.

"I've been keeping an eye," Alan defended, though the set of his shoulders spoke of his own doubts. "But you're right. Maybe I should look at him again. A lot has come up now that we weren't anticipating, though."

Kathleen sighed. "Alan, I'm going to ask one more time. Do you think your closeness to these kids, to the Westpooles- is clouding your judgment in this case?"

It was a question loaded with the weight of responsibility, of lives in the balance and futures uncertain. Alan's eyes, aged with years of service and secrets, met Kathleen's, understanding her as a colleague needing to ask the same desperate question a second time.

But it still pissed him off.

"You dare ask me that, Kathleen?" His voice, usually so sure, cracked like a whip. His calm demeanor was splintering. "After everything we've been through, after all I've done to keep this town and its people safe?"

Kathleen, taken aback by the vehemence in his response, stood her ground. But inside that steadfast resolve, a twinge of regret pulled at her. This was Alan- her friend and her confidant- but he was also the sheriff, the man the town turned to in times of crisis.

"Alan, I didn't mean to—"

"No, I get it. Question the man who's dedicated his life to justice, huh? Question his integrity?" Alan's sarcasm was a bitter coat over the raw hurt in his eyes. He jabbed a finger toward her, the betrayal he felt lending him a frenetic energy. "But let's not forget, Kathleen, it was you who marched into this very station, fire in your eyes, accusin' me of pinning Ruby's murder on the wrong man when I had Joel behind bars. You were so sure of it, weren't you?"

Her mouth opened, a retort or maybe an apology on her lips, but Alan was far from done.

"No, I don't need to stand here and justify myself. Not to you, not to anyone."

With that, Alan turned, his stride heavy with anger. The door to the station slammed with a finality that left a ringing silence in its wake.

Kathleen stood there, amidst the echoes of their argument and the lingering scent of Alan's cologne.

As Alan's cruiser roared to life outside and peeled away from the curb, Kathleen couldn't help but feel a fracture had formed — in their friendship, in their united front, and in the very foundation of the peace they had vowed to rebuild in Adelaide.

And there, in the cooling air of the deserted station, Kathleen was once again reminded of the fragility of trust and the heavy cost of truth in a world that was as unforgiving as it was unpredictable.

Chapter Eighteen

The day Adelaide organized the search for Christopher was one painted with an anxious gray- the kind where the sun seemed hesitant to rise, as if it, too, feared what might be found in its light.

Our town, typically abuzz with the mundane happenings of everyday life, was now united in a palpable tension. The adults, normally so composed, seemed to fray at the edges with their concerns bleeding out in hushed tones and tight-lipped expressions.

We, the children, were mere observers to the day's somber proceedings. Our understanding of the situation was limited, kept on the periphery of the truth, shielded by well-meaning lies.

"Stay inside," they told us, their words stern but eyes betraying a fear they couldn't hide. "It's important you're safe." Safe from what, though, they wouldn't say.

I remember watching Erik as he peered out his window, his usual buoyancy deflated and replaced with only quiet.

. "They're gonna bring Chris back," he muttered, more to himself than anyone, clinging to a sliver of hope like a lifeline.

Brittany, though, with her ever-present realism, understood more than any of us did.

"They're not looking for Chris alive," she said, the weight of her words far too heavy for her young age. It was a truth we couldn't grasp then- a foresight we'd only fully understand in the years to come. But she was right. They weren't searching for a boy who was hiding or lost- they were searching for a body.

As the day wore on, a restless energy settled over us. We were too young to comprehend the situation fully, yet old enough to sense that our lives were changing irrevocably and profoundly.

That understanding became crystal clear when news trickled back to town, not of Christopher's discovery–but of Monte's.

Monte the pervert- the man whispered about in hushed, ominous tones-had been found. But it wasn't an arrest. It was a recovery.

His body lay at the edge of Pichol Creek. It was Miss Patty, a local grocer of stout build and usually unflappable nature who stumbled upon him.

Her scream, they said, echoed through the woods like a banshee crying out. It was a chilling sound that marked the end of one mystery and the deepening of another.

Miss Patty's hands trembled as she recounted the scene to the authorities. "He was just layin' there, all bloated up with eyes open to the sky like he was askin' God why," she repeated to anyone who'd listen for days after the discovery. Her own eyes were haunted by an image that would never leave her.

The description of Monte's gruesome body became our newfound nightmare and left us all shaken.

Others would talk about how his blood, thick and drying, clung to his pale skin, lending an eerie sheen to his lifeless form. There were no visible wounds except for one-a single gunshot wound in the center of his forehead. The absence of a gun nearby only deepened the mystery, casting shadows of doubt and fear upon our town.

With Monte's discovery, the murmurs grew louder and more urgent. Speculations ran rampant, filling in the gaps of the unknown with theories whispered fervently along Adelaide's streets. The word "murder" was spoken with a frequency that made us all shudder.

That night, as shadows stretched across our rooms and the murmurs from our parents' televisions hummed like distant thunder, Erik, Josh, Brittany, and I were united in a shared, unspoken understanding.

Our world had shifted, twisted into a narrative we couldn't escape. Monsters, we realized, weren't confined to the folklore or stories I'd devoured in books. They existed in our town and in our lives.

And I laid there, grappling with private fears, I understood that the boundary between innocence and the harsh truths of the adult world had been crossed, and there would be no turning back for any of us.

Monte's lifeless body at Pichol Creek wasn't

just the end of his story, though.

It was the beginning of another.

Chapter Nineteen

Good ol' Jimmy Carel was a familiar face around town, though not exactly for the best reasons. Jimmy was known far and wide for his scruffy beard, always tangled with crumbs and whatever else he'd managed to find in his latest dumpster dive. His clothes were a patchwork quilt of stains and holes, and I reckon they'd seen more seasons than the clothes of most folks in our town.

Jimmy had a way of tottering about that made you think the ground was swaying beneath him. His walk was more of a shuffle, really, like he had a secret dance with the sidewalk that nobody else knew about.

He'd often be seen talking to the air or taking long, aimless strolls through the woods, chasing after some phantom of his own imagination.

Now, when it came to shoes, Jimmy wasn't too choosy. He'd wear whatever he could scrounge up, often sporting mismatched pairs that looked like they'd been rescued from the bottom of a lake. They were soaked and muddied, and sometimes, he'd lose one along the way just like it had run off on its own adventure.

He also had a habit of collecting' things, especially shiny bits and bobs he'd find lying around town. He'd stuff his pockets full of them and it was a common sight to see him proudly displaying his treasures to anyone who'd listen.

Of course, most folks just nodded and smiled,

humoring him as he rambled on.

I wish I could tell you that Jimmy's story was one of redemption, but truth be told, he was known as a local drug addict-a victim of his own demons- and that's exactly what would kill him some years later.

JImmy's story is a sad tale that our town witnessed unfold over the years, and it cast a shadow over the otherwise colorful character he'd once been.

It was Jimmy, though, who stumbled upon Monte's truck that morning after the body was found.

He added a touch of grit to an already somber scene.

It was a crisp morning when Alan received that fateful phone call, beckoning him to the old mine.

Monte's pickup truck-the very contraption that used to ferry him through the winding roads of our secluded woods, had been found abandoned.

Now, as an adult looking back and remembering, I can't help but conjure the image of that dilapidated mine and the eerie feeling that hung heavy around it. My memories, tainted by the darkness of the past, cast long shadows across the overgrown entrance, hiding the remnants of a time when coal mining had been the heartbeat of our town.

Alan arrived at that spot, his face bearing the weight of uncertainty, and stood solitary and forlorn staring at the forsaken truck.

The inside of that truck, as it's been described to me, held an eerie emptiness. There were no signs of scuffle and no hints at how Monte ended up miles away with a hole in his head.

Alan decided to venture inside the old mine. The entrance seemed to swallow him whole as he stepped into the cavernous darkness, his flashlight casting eerie shadows on the damp walls.

The air inside was stale and heavy, and it clung to him as he cautiously made his way deeper into the cavern. Each step echoed through the tunnel with a lonely sound that reverberated with the weight of his uncertainty.

As he ventured further, his flashlight's beam illuminated a sight that sent a chill down his spine—a large puddle of blood staining the rocky ground. It gleamed like a macabre mirror, reflecting the fear in Alan's heart.

Alan knelt down to inspect the crimson pool, his mind racing with grim possibilities.

As he investigated, desperation clung to him like the very darkness of the mine and he knew he had to press on. With each step, his determination grew stronger- his resolve to find answers was unwavering.

Yet, as he delved deeper into the labyrinthine passages, there was still no sign of Chris or Ellen. The mine seemed to hold its secrets close, taunting him with its ominous silence. Alan's flashlight continued to pierce the gloom, revealing only the desolate emptiness of the tunnels.

He called out, his voice echoing through the caverns, hoping for a response, but there was no answer-only the distant drip of water and the haunting echoes of his own words.

Chapter Twenty

That same night, Erik and I managed to sneak back down to Pichol Creek, defying our mothers' stern warnings. We had fallen asleep and failed to capture the nereids on our first attempt. We would do better this time..

As we stood by the creek's edge, the moon's soft glow painted shimmering ripples on the dark waters and the world was cloaked in an inky veil.

Our flashlights were like small beacons of determination in the face of what lay ahead. It was a place we weren't meant to be, and our mothers were likely to wear our hides right off if they caught us back down there.

Erik, bless his heart, took the risk anyway, and together, we dared to confront those wicked mermaids.

As we scanned the moonlit shadows, the woods seemed to breathe with secrets, casting eerie shapes that danced over the trees. In that breathless moment, we caught sight of a figure emerging from the depths of the forest.

Fear took hold of me, and I gripped Erik's arm. Our eyes locked on the approaching silhouette.

It was none other than Steven, a former friend of Ruby's who had tended bar at Rowdy's, our town's watering hole. Yet, something was amiss tonight—something that filled the air with an unsettling tension. Bloodstains marred his clothes, and his eyes, once familiar, now held the weight of the world's darkest secrets.

"Erik?" I heard myself whisper, my voice quivering like a fawn taking its first steps.

Steven halted in his tracks, his gaze flitting around the woods, looking for the source of my whisper.

. "Who's out there?" he murmured. All at once, he caught us in his gaze.

"That you, Tessie?" he asked, recognizing me. He didn't seem to know who Erik was.

"Girl, What in tarnation are y'all doin' out here?"

The urgency in his voice sent a shiver down my spine. "We're lookin' for Christopher," I replied, my voice barely more than a breath. "He's gone missing and we got this notion that some nereids done took him."

Steven's brow furrowed in a way that hinted at something deeper than confusion and he cast uneasy glances around the moonlit clearing.

"Y'all need to high-tail it outta here," he urged, his words heavy with desperation. "This ain't a place for youngins tonight. I assume your mamas don't know you're here so I won't say nothin' about seeing you if you don't say nothin' about seeing me. Deal?"

My eyes couldn't help but be drawn to the bloodstains that marred Steven's clothes. It was a detail too sinister to ignore.

"Steven," I asked cautiously, my twang-tinged words barely rising above the night's whispers. "Are you bleeding?"

He hesitated, his gaze fixed on me like he was running through every possible lie he could tell all at once. "Nah, honey.. I been lookin' for—" He paused, struggling to find the right words.

"I been lookin' for Christopher, too," he finally said, his voice carrying a burden too heavy for the moonlit night.

"I'll keep looking. I'll let y'all know if I find anything. Y'all need to leave, though, and don't you dare come back here."

In that moment, I couldn't help but wonder if there was more to Steven's story than met the eye. Had he encountered the nereids? Or was there something else lurking in the shadows of our town, something darker and more mysterious than even the most twisted folktales?

We did as Steven asked and left the woods, but Erik convinced me that we needed to tell someone about what we'd witnessed out there under the frog songs and moonlight..

Bloodstains and all.

Chapter Twenty-One

Erik and I pedaled furiously toward town. Our bikes rattled along the dusty road as the relentless heat of the summer night soaked our clothes in sweat, leaving us breathless by the time we reached the sheriff station.

We tumbled off our bikes, our chests heaving, and ran inside, clamoring for a grown-up.

Kathleen, unable to sleep, had come into the station to give Ruby's file another read-through. She was just getting there as we pulled up and stood at the station's entrance as she turned her attention toward us, genuine curiosity etching its way across her face, mingled with growing concern.

Gasping for breath, we tried to explain why we'd come in such a hurried mess. "Miss Kathleen," Erik wheezed, his voice quivering. "There's somethin' you need to know about."

Kathleen's gaze focused on us, her eyes narrowing with concentration as she awaited our tale. "What is it, you two?" she inquired, her voice patient yet tinged with an air of anticipation. "And what are you doing running around out here? It's the middle of the damn night!

Between heaving breaths, we began to recount our creek-side encounter—Steven's bloodstained clothes, the haunting look in his eyes, and the way he told us to not tell on him and he wouldn't tell on us.

As Kathleen listened intently, her supermodel features underwent a gradual transformation from curiosity to one of resolute determination. She absorbed our words like the detective she was, meticulously assembling the intricate pieces of a perplexing puzzle. In that moment, the world seemed to hold its breath, poised on the brink of her epiphany.

Disappointingly, once our hurried narrative had run its course, though, only went to scolding us. "You two need to steer clear of that creek," she asserted. Her serious, steely tone sent a shiver coursing down my spine.

"But, Miss Kathleen," I stammered, still grappling to regain my breath. "We've got to find Christopher. We can't just—" My words trailed off as her unwavering gaze bore down on me, leaving me momentarily speechless.

"No," she said firmly. "You must stay far away from that creek."

She then turned toward the desk and sat down, pulling the phone over closer to her.

Erik and I exchanged anxious glances, realizing that we were about to be punished worse than either of us had ever dreamed. She was calling our mothers.

"Miss Kathleen," I implored. "Please, there's no need to call our parents. We won't do it again, I promise."

Erik chimed in. His voice was trembling in fear of what lay ahead. "Yeah, please, Miss Kathleen," he added. "We won't go near that creek anymore. My mama worked today. She's tired. Let her sleep!"

Kathleen's expression softened for a moment as she gazed at our youthful, remorseful faces. It was evident that she understood the childish fear that gripped our young hearts.

However, Kathleen firmly replied, "I'm sorry, but I have to let your parents know where you are. It's important they know what happened."

With a heavy heart, she turned her attention to her duty, looking up our parents' numbers in the directory. Erik's father arrived first, walking through the doors with a scowl that would make a grown man cower. I could only imagine the scolding that awaited Erik when they left.

Mama arrived shortly after. In contrast to Erik's dad, her eyes filled with a mix of relief and frustration as she stood, quiet in the doorway, and looked me up and down. "Tessie, what in the hell were you thinkin', runnin' off into the woods at night like that?" she scolded, her voice tinged with a mother's worry. "How many times do we all have to keep telling you kids? Christopher's missing! Do you want to be missing, too?"

She grabbed my hand, then turned and offered Kathleen a quick parting thanks as she pulled me out the door and gestured for me to get in the truck.

Erik's dad loaded my bike into the bed for Mama and gave her a polite, but unfriendly nod as he got back into his own car and readied to drive off.

As we drove home, I couldn't help but dread the impending scolding and grounding that awaited me once Charlie got in on it.

This had been a bad decision, I thought to myself. We'd have been better off taking our chances with Steven.

Chapter Twenty-Two

As I stood there in my room, surrounded by the dusty, well-thumbed pages of my cherished monster books, a heavy feeling settled upon my little heart. That summer had been a load a ten-year-old heart ain't meant to bear. The afternoon sun slipped through the tattered curtains, casting its warm, golden light upon the cluttered shelves that held my most prized possessions.

My little brother, Devin, stood in the doorway, his eyes fixed on the scene I was carrying out in front of him.
"Tessie?" he asked, his voice pure innocence. "You already caught all them monsters in them books?"

Turning toward him, I felt the sting of unshed tears clouding my vision, emotions I hadn't realized were so close to the surface.

"No, Devin," I said, my voice trembling. "But there ain't no such thing as all the stupid pretend monsters in these books. The only monsters in this world are people with bad hearts. I don't need these anymore."

My hand swept across the worn pages, each one filled with tales of creatures that had long danced on the edges of my imagination, blurring the lines between fantasy and what was real. As I gave each book one last flip-through, I tossed it unceremoniously into an old fruit box I'd found down at the municipal dumpster.

I was throwing my books away and leaving behind all that silliness once and for all.

Devin's dirty little face wrinkled in confusion, his brow furrowing like a row in a fresh-plowed field.

"But Tessie," he said. "You love your books."

Sinking down onto my bed, the weight of the world settling upon my shoulders, I whispered, "Not anymore, Devin. I hate 'em. They ain't nothin' but lies."

Devin's eyes searched mine, his innocence seeking answers in the depths of my ten-years of acquired wisdom.

But how could he ever understand the shadows I'd glimpsed? All the knowledge that had been stealing away at my innocence?

He was too young to understand such things, yet in his own tender way, he reached out to me, wrapping his tiny arms around my waist. His embrace held the warmth of a little brother's love, a comforting balm for the ache in my heart.

"Will you take a nap with me?" he asked. "I'm tired and you'll feel better, too."

He was right. I was tired.

I nodded and together we climbed up on my bed, pulling my worn out quilt over us as we drifted into slumber, his small frame nestled against mine.

The room darkened as clouds gathered outside, ready to pour rain out over the trees.

We woke hungry to the smell of Mama frying pork chops. My eyes fluttered open, greeted by the gentle rays of sunlight streaming through the window. The rain had passed along with my sour mood.

Yet it wasn't the sunlight that drew my bleary gaze; it was the sight of my beloved monster books, all neat and stacked back up on the shelves.

I knew Mama hadn't touched 'em, and Devin was still too little to reach that high. Then, that's when I caught a whiff of Nana Carter's sweet lavender perfume, lingerin' in the air like a fond memory.

My heart swelled with gratitude and a touch of awe as I pieced together what had happened. Nana Carter, my wise and loving grandmother, must've ventured out to that old trash can to rescue my precious books from their fate.

At that moment, I understood the depth of Nana Carter's love and understanding. She'd seen the hurt in my heart, the loss of my childhood daydreaming, and in her own special way, she'd tried to mend it.

As I looked up at my tidied book shelf, I knew that monsters, both real and make-believe, would forever be a part of our world. But I also saw the goodness, love, and courage dwelling within the hearts of those who cared for us-those who tried to shield us from the darkness- would, too.

Nana Carter had fought the monsters, herself, and refused to let them take a piece of who I was.

It was a lesson I'd carry with me through the rest of my life's journey-a testament to the strength of family and the everlasting' power of a Nana's love.

Chapter Twenty-Three

The days that followed the discovery of Monte's blood in that old mine and traces of Chris's blood and hair in his truck were filled with a heavy sense of dread that settled over Adelaide like a blanket of fog. It was as if the very air had thickened with a foreboding, and the townsfolk were left grappling with a tangled web of secrets and mysteries that had chilled us all with fear.

Alan had been burning the midnight oil, pouring over the clues and trying to make sense of the perplexing puzzle.

When the lab reports finally came in, it was like a thunderclap on a still summer night, jolting the town from its uneasy slumber. The confirmation that Monte's blood had been found in that dark, foreboding mine sent shivers down spines, and the old mine that had once let us all down, spinning Adelaide from a bustling community to a hub of impoverished despair had now bore the stain of yet another tragedy.

I remember the day Alan called for a press conference at the small, timeworn sheriff's station.

He opened it to the public and, of course, Mama took me down there to see what the news might be about Christopher.

She'd gotten over the notion that she should shield me from the horrors going on. If I wouldn't listen to her about staying out of those woods, she'd have me hear every dirty detail until I was scared to even think about heading back down Pichol Creek trail without a grown up.

The room felt cramped, and the dusty sunbeams that filtered through the worn-out windows did little to alleviate the heaviness that hung in the air. The folks settled into their creaky chairs, their faces etched with worry and anticipation.

Alan cleared his throat. His expression was grave, and began to lay it all out.

"Folks," he said, his voice as serious as a hound on a scent. "I'm sure you've heard the rumors around town and it's true. The lab results are in. That blood we found in the mine—it's Monte's, no doubt about it."

A collective murmur rippled through the room, like the rustling of leaves in a brisk autumn wind.

But Alan wasn't finished. He continued, his words gathering in the air of the room like storm clouds.

"There's more to this, though.. Like you may also have heard, there were traces of the Kendler boy found in Monte's truck, which was abandoned out at the mine. We believe Monte was killed out there, then left where he was found out in the woods. There were no traces of Christopher in the mine, though. If he was in Monte's truck, and we believe he was, we can't be for certain how long ago it was or if he was at the mine when Monte was killed."

He paused, allowing the gravity of his words to settle in.

The room fell into a hushed silence, broken only by the sound of Debbie Kendler weeping into her cardigan sleeves..

I would later hear tell that, in the quiet of his office, away from prying eyes, Alan had already spent a morning sitting, staring at the reports, sobbing just as hard.

Now, I know grown-ups try to keep their worries from us kids, but we ain't blind, and we sure ain't dumb. I looked around and could see it in their eyes, hear it in their hushed voices when they thought I wasn't listening'. And I reckon I just sensed it too, even back then, though I was just a youngin'.

The belief that Chris was long was hung thick all around us.

That night, I was restless. From my bed, I could hear the wind whispering' secrets through the trees, and the moonlight cast long, eerie shadows that danced like specters in the dark. It was as if the whole world was holding its breath, waitin' for someone to scream.

I can't help but think that Alan, sittin' in his office, starin' at the reports, was waitin' too.

Waitin' for some sign- some clue that would lead him to Chris, alive and well.

I reckon deep down, he knew it was a long

shot, and the fear that Chris had been taken from us forever was one that weighed heavy on his shoulders.

But even as scared as we all were- it was a gentle kind of fear.

A fear that reminds us that sometimes, in the darkest of times, hope is the only thing that keeps us goin'.

Chapter Twenty-Four

One day, right in the midst of this whole Monte business, Alan got a phone call from his past.

It was from a woman named Carol. She's the one folks back in Sanders couldn't help but gossip about.

You see, she was at the center of the scandal that had folks pointing fingers at Alan, questioning his judgment.

Carol had seen him on the news when she caught wind of the mess unraveling in Adelaide. I can only imagine how that must've hit him, like a slap in the face from a ghost.

Mama always said the last thing a man needs when he's knee-deep in troubles is a reminder of the troubles he's left behind.

I can't rightly say what they talked about on that phone call, because I of course wasn't privy to their words.

I heard that Alan had a weariness in his voice when he was talking to her though and that he asked Carol not to contact him again. He'd been careful putting up that wall between the past and present and he had no desire whatsoever to knock it back down for her.

I reckon we all got ghosts from our pasts- things we'd rather leave buried.

Alan, well, he had his share of ghosts, that's for sure. But that call from Carol was like the ghosts had come back to haunt him, right when he was facing a whole new kind of trouble.

Realizings he'd heard what was going on all the way down in Georgie hit like a thunderclap. Our quiet little town was making headlines, and that couldn't have been easy for Alan. He had his hands full trying to solve multiple mysteries, and now was having to deal publicly with the weight of his past, too.

But Alan was a stubborn one, and he didn't let that call from Carol shake him for too long. He had a mess to sort out and was running a town that was gripped by fear.

So when he told Carol not to contact him again, he made sure to drive home to her that he had enough on his plate, enough troubles to keep him up at night, and had long since had enough of her.

Kathleen, the beautiful state investigator who had come in from Richmond to help, paid close attention as she eavesdropped on that call- and her interest in how he handled his ex, it would later turn out, had very little to do with the job.

Now, as I've heard it, Kathleen's had developed a fondness for Alan in their time working together and despite some animosity over butting heads while investigating together, she didn't wanna let any negative tension between 'em linger.

From what I was told, she walked right up to Alan, and reached out to touch his hand.

That touch must have thrown sparks, because from that day on, you couldn't be in the same room as those two without noticing that if they looked at each other a flicker of something' more than just friendship lit up both sets of eyes.

It's a funny thing that in times of trouble, when the world feels like it's spinning out of control, sometimes two hearts find each other just like two rusty old fish hooks getting themselves all tangled up in the filth of an old tackle box.

Chapter Twenty-Five

It was a few days after Kathleen and Alan had that moment of mending fences that I'd reel Charlie's rusty old fish hook heart into the beginning of a new discovery.

I was sitting at the supper table with my family with the TV humming in the background.

The news anchor mentioned Adelaide as his voice dropped heavy like they do when they're about to lay something nasty on you. It hung in the air like a storm cloud, brewing up something awful and the table fell to a hush except Mallory's babbling over squishing her peas as the rest of us waited to find out what was about to be said.

The news anchor rattled on.

"According to early morning reports from the VBI, the status of young Christopher Kendler's case has been changed from search and rescue to recovery, with state investigators no longer believing the young boy will be found alive."

It had been over a week since he disappeared into the shadows of the woods, and with the new evidence of blood and hair in Monte's truck, hope had faded like a cracked lantern in the wind.

Joel quickly hurried to grab the TV remote off the back of the couch and flicked the TV off in a panic, but it was too late. Tears welled up in my eyes, threatening to spill over, but I blinked 'em back.

I couldn't let Devin or Mallory see me cryin' like that-not when Devin had put on a brave face for me.

But inside, my heart was heavy, weighed down by the pain of losing one of my best friends.

I couldn't help but think 'bout all them times we'd laughed and played, our voices ringing through them woods like echoes of our youth. And now, there was just silence, a hollowness in my heart that threatened to consume me.

As the TV continued to drone on, my family exchanged glances, their eyes filled with sorrow. My mama reached over and squeezed my hand, her touch offering me some small comfort in that moment of darkness.

I couldn't help but wonder if the Nereids, the mythical creatures I'd been so obsessed with, had truly taken Christopher away, lured by his youth and innocence. It was a painful thought, one that filled me with anger and sadness all at once.

But deep down, I knew that monsters weren't the real threat. People, with their dark desires and hidden secrets, they were the ones who could truly hurt us. And as I looked at my family, tryin' to hold on to hope even as it slipped through our fingers, I realized that sometimes, the most terrifying monsters of all wore human faces.

As I sat there at the supper table, the weight

of that dreadful news pressing down on my heart, I couldn't hold back the flood of emotions that surged within me. The tears that had been threatening' earlier now welled up in my eyes, overflowing' like a river bursting' its banks. My world was crumbling around me, and I couldn't bear the thought of losing Christopher, my best friend.

With a quivering' voice, I turned to Charlie, his weathered face showing signs of the burden we all carried. He'd been volunteering with the search every day and driving around late at night, wracking his brain trying to figure out where Christopher might be.

"Don't stop looking, please," I pleaded with all the desperation a young heart could muster. "Please keep lookin' for him."

Unable to hold back my crying anymore, I could feel the tears streaming down my cheeks, their salty taste spoiling my supper.

Charlie's eyes met mine and I saw a mix of sorrow and helplessness mirrored back at me.

He reached out and gently squeezed my shoulder, his touch offering me what little comfort he could provide.

My mama, sitting beside me, placed a hand on my other shoulder, her eyes filled with tears that matched my own. She didn't need words to convey her love and shared pain-her touch spoke volumes.

But as much as my heart ached and my tears

flowed, I couldn't accept the idea that Christopher was gone. He was my best friend-my partner in all my craziest adventures- and I couldn't bear to imagine a world without him in it.

I knew deep down that the odds were stacked against us and that the experts on the TV were likely right. But hope is a powerful thing, especially in the heart of a child.

So, I clung to it, desperately willing it to be true, willing Christopher to come walking out of those woods, safe and sound.

Charlie cleared his throat. "We ain't givin' up hope, Tessie. Me and Joel will keep lookin' for him.

He looked across the table at Joel, whose own worry-worn eyes raised up to meet mine with a slow nod. "For as long as it takes," he added. "We won't stop until we know for sure. Just like we'll keep on looking for the Dewey girl. There's too much lost out there right now for anyone to be giving up."

Mama nodded and pulled me into a tight hug.

"I won't stop prayin' for him either," she said, her voice shaky but filled with determination. "I'll pray every night that he comes back to us."

And with that, we made a silent promise- a vow that echoed through the walls of our home. We wouldn't give up-not as long as there was even a glimmer of it left to be found deep in our tired hearts.

We finished our supper, each bite a

bittersweet reminder of the empty chairs left sitting that night at the Kendler and Dewey tables.

Chapter Twenty-Six

Charlie and Joel were brothers bound by blood and a fierce determination to get each other through whatever bullshit this life tossed at them. They'd always done everything together and together, they weren't about to give up the hunt for Adelaide's missing children.

They scoured every corner of our town, turned over every lead, and weren't afraid to trespass to peer through the time-worn windows of old houses and sheds they found peppered along the countryside.

The whole town was gripped by a collective fear and sorrow, like a storm that refused to pass, but Charlie and Joel were like the calm in the eye of that tempest. Their resolve to bring Christopher home was unshakeable, and Ellen Dewey had fallen into their radar by association.

One evening as the sun was setting in shades of orange and pink looking like rainbow sherbert, Charlie and Joel were filling up the truck and getting ready to come home when they ran into Crazy Jimmy.

"Just who I want to see!" he hollered. "The Westpoole brothers! I hear y'all are the holdouts on the search for the Kendler boy!"

"I don't think we're the only ones," Charlie said, more hoping than knowing.

"Well I was wonderin' if anyone had told you

all about those old cisterns behind Monte's house?"
Jimmy asked.

"If it's on Monte's property, I'm sure it's been
searched already," Joel said with a sigh. He didn't have
much patience for Crazy Jimmy.

"I reckon they ain't!" Jimmy said. "Monte laid
grass over most of them. Most folk don't even know
they're out there, but that's where Monte's daddy
used to hide his moonshine and I know for a fact that
there's one Monte used to drop all those dead critters
into after he got done doin' God knows what to 'em,
because when I've been without a roof I used to go
out there and sleep in some of them cisterns and I
happened across a pile of rotting cats and dogs and
what have you one time and never did go back."

"Did you tell the police this?" Charlie asked,
bewildered by what he was hearing.

"Of course not!" Jimmy laughed. "Sheeeit,
Charlie! You think I'm gonna cop to trespassing and
squatting on someone else's place? I'm telling you
now!"

"You know where these cisterns are?" Charlie
asked. "You want to come out and show us?"

"Oooh no," Jimmy said, shaking his head and
backing up a step. "You won't catch me out there in
those woods. But I can tell you where a few of 'em are
at! They's easy to find if you know what to look for."

Charlie reached into his truck and grabbed a
memo pad and a pen and together he and Jimmy

worked through the property, making note of a few places to look for kicked up sod and metal cistern lids underneath.

Despite the fact that they'd been on their way home to fill their hungry bellies, Charlie and Joel decided they didn't want to waste any time. We'd all been made aware recently of how time was a merciless thing, and every moment wasted was a moment that could make all the difference.

So, as the sun started to dip below the horizon, they headed to Monte's end of the woods for one last look around.

Chapter Twenty-Seven

Meanwhile, back in Adelaide, Kathleen wasn't one to let things rest- especially when it came to finding the truth. After hearing about us seeing Steven in the woods covered in blood, she knew she had to pay him a visit and find out if there was anything more to the story than met the eye.

She'd waited a few days, giving him time to think he'd gotten away with anything we might have caught him doing. She knew from her years of experience that the only way to catch someone in a tale is to catch them off guard. Just when he thought he'd gotten away with whatever, she'd pop up and ask him questions, shaking the truth out of him with the vibrato of his own nerves.

When she knocked on Steven's door, he answered meekly, seeming like a shadow of his former self.

Steven's eyes, once full of smartassery and bravado, now held a somber weight.

"Steven," Kathleen began, her voice gentle but persistent. "You don't know me. I'm Kathleen Quinn. I work for the state and I'm here in town helping Sheriff Cline with the missing people. Can I come in?"

Steven sighed, shaking his head as he stepped out on the porch, motioning toward the patio chairs. "We can sit here," he said. "What's this about?"

Kathleen smiled warmly, but squinted her

eyes, making note of his inhospitality as she sat down out on the dirty porch furniture.

"I heard something about some kids seeing you out in the woods, covered in blood," she said, getting straight to the point. "Mind if we talk about it?"

Steven's gaze shifted, his eyes briefly darting away from Kathleen's inquisitive stare. He hesitated for a moment, as if weighing' his options, before finally stepping' nodding slow.

He shifted uncomfortably in his chair, his gaze avoiding Kathleen's piercing eyes.

"It's nothin', really," he mumbled, his voice barely above a whisper. "I was just skinning a deer. Got a bit messy, is all."

Kathleen shook her head.

"Steven," Kathleen pressed on, her tone firmer now. "Those bruises on your face and neck don't look like they came from skinnin' a deer. What really happened?"

Steven hesitated again as every muscle in his body locked, tense, like he was getting ready to jump up and make a run for it.

Finally, he let out a heavy sigh and relaxed.

"I got into a fight at the bar," he said, his eyes finally meeting Kathleen's.

Kathleen leaned forward, her expression one of genuine concern. "Which bar, Steven?"

"Rowdy's," he said.

Rowdy's. The same bar where he worked- the same bar where Ruby had been a regular.

Kathleen's mind raced, trying to connect the dots between Steven, Ruby, and the events that had unfolded in Adelaide recently. She knew there was more to this story than met the eye, and she was determined to unravel it, now thinking Steven must be sitting right at the center of it all.

Determined to squeeze every last drop of information from Steven, she gained a fire in her eyes. She was ready to wrestle' with the devil himself, if she had to, and pin him to the mat.

Steven, on the other hand, was like a cat caught in a corner, his back against the wall, and no way out. He was sweating bullets, trying to come up with answers that wouldn't incriminate him.

But Kathleen wasn't havin' none of that.

"Steven," she said, her voice calm yet persistent. "I understand you've been through a lot, but I need to know what happened out there. People are missing, and we need to find them."

Steven laid his head back and shut his eyes as he breathed heavier. He finally spoke, his voice shaky, "I swear, Kathleen, I had nothin' to do with those missing kids. And when Ruby...when Ruby disappeared, the cops kept harassin' me- I've been accused so many times of things I ain't never done. Things I'd never do. You know Cline, right? You can ask him. I don't even like women."

Kathleen's brow furrowed in confusion. "Steven, there was never a missing person's report filed for Ruby. Everybody thought she just up and left town. Remember? And who's accused you of what now? As far as I know, you've been off the radar on all this for a good while."

For a moment, Steven looked like he'd swallowed a mouthful of nails. His lips pressed together in a thin line, and he clammed up, as if a mile of open road had manifested between them.

"I can't talk about this," he said. "And I won't-not unless you come with a warrant and my lawyer."

He got up and walked back in the house, slamming the door behind him.

Kathleen's face flashed hot in fury. Steven wasn't giving up any more information. He'd said his piece, and he wasn't about to say another word.

Though frustrated, she knew when to pick her battles, and she realized that she wouldn't be getting any more out of Steven that day.

So, she left his place, her mind still racing with questions and suspicions. The more she dug, the deeper the mysteries seemed to get.

Kathleen knew she was treading on dangerous

ground, uncovering secrets that had been buried for a long time-but she was a woman with a mission, and she wasn't about to let those secrets stay buried.

Chapter Twenty-Eight

The day was waning in the dense forest behind Monte's old place. The air was thick with tension, each rustle of leaves or snap of twigs beneath Charlie's feet echoing like a distant cry for help.

A nagging feeling had driven him and Joel out to explore the woods and check those old cisterns Crazy Jimmy had mentioned.

With a flashlight gripped tightly in his hand and a heavy heart, Charlie inched closer to one of the cisterns- Joel having ventured off to another.

He couldn't predict what horrors might await him down there and he'd already been warned that at least one of them was seemingly full of dead cats, but he knew he had to look.

He couldn't let me down. He'd promised to keep looking, so keep looking he would.

As his flashlight pierced the oppressive darkness of the cistern, it revealed a chilling sight that made his heart plummet.

Huddled in the bottom, barely visible, was the pale, curled up body of Christopher Kendler.

As the flashlight trailed across his face, Christopher's head moved toward the light, weakly. He looked as though he'd seen a ghost, his frail form dirtied and battered and his wide eyes reflecting an unspoken terror. A pang of anguish gripped Charlie's chest at the sight and he rushed down the half ladder and dropped to the boy's side, his voice quivering.

"Chris! It's Charlie Westpoole! Hang on. We're here to get you out. You're safe now."

As he looked around, taking in the muddy cistern bottom, he was struck by an odd realization that Christopher was surrounded in white and brown feathers, though there wasn't a bird of any kind in sight- not even bones.

Christopher was in no condition to speak. He trembled uncontrollably, his lips a sickly shade of blue from the cold.

Charlie realized they needed to act swiftly and shouted for Joel, who was nearby, to come quickly. Charlie knew he couldn't carry the boy out of the cistern on his own, and he couldn't bear to leave him alone for a moment longer.

Joel arrived at the cistern, his breaths coming in frantic gasps as he looked down and saw the grim scene.

"Head to the house and call Alan!" Charlie said. "Tell him to send an ambulance. The boy's barely hanging on!"

As Joel dashed off to make the call, Charlie remained with Chris, his heart heavy with worry and a growing sense of dread. Christopher's condition was dire, and Charle thought for certain he'd die right there in his arms.

Charlie turned his attention back to the feathers scattered around the cistern. They seemed out of place in a stark contrast to the grimness of the situation. His skin crawled, and he shivered as he tried to make sense of the bizarre and unsettling scene that had unfolded before him.

Charlie knew that whatever had happened to Chris out in those woods was far more sinister than he could have ever imagined.

Back at the house, the hushed telephone conversation between Joel and the sheriff unfolded as Mama and I strained to catch every word.

Joel's voice was tight with anxiety as he spoke into the phone, the urgency in his tone unmistakable.

Mama listened, wide eyed. She clutched her hands together, her knuckles white, as I crawled up under her arms for comfort. We couldn't make sense of it all. He said something about a cistern and something about feathers and- most notably- that Christopher was alive, but just barely.

It didn't take long for Joel to finish the call. He rushed out the door, leaving it open as he raced to meet the sheriff and guide him to Christopher and Charlie.

The urgency in his movements- the tension etched into the lines on his face—were impossible to miss. I watched him go, my heart heavy with concern for my best friend and the terror he must have endured out there in the woods.

As Mama and I listened to Nana walk over and slam the door shut, I couldn't help but think about the stories I'd read– the tales of mythical creatures and beings who, rather than carry on monstrously, watched over those in need.

And as I heard the faint rumble of thunder in the distance, a thought landed sweetly on my mind.

With wide eyes and a sense of wonder, I whispered to Mama.

"Mama, I think Chris was protected by a Thunderbird."

Chapter Twenty-Nine

As the days slowly rolled on, Christopher's hospital room became a hub for the investigation- nobody wanting to stray too far from the miracle of Chris's survival.

Sunshine streamed through the window, casting warm, golden streaks of light that danced on the pale, sterile walls. Our little corner of the world held its breath, teetering between hope and despair.

Ellen Dewey was still missing. Ruby was still dead.

But Chris had made it.

In that room, beneath the flickering fluorescence, Christopher lay in his hospital bed like a weary traveler returning from a perilous journey.

As he recovered and regained strength, every word and every gesture seemed to carry a heavy weight.

Christopher, his young voice barely a whisper, lay trembling with the memories of his harrowing ordeal.

As Kathleen listened intently, he began to recount the fragments of his chilling story.

He spoke of the moment Monte had snatched him from his bike and the impact that had sent his head crashing against the unforgiving ground.

His memories were fragmented, though, like scattered pieces of a jigsaw puzzle, and yet they were filled with all the hope in the world.

He had seen Ellen, the missing girl, alive.

In the darkness of Monte's sinister world, Ellen had existed as a fragile beacon of hope amidst the shadows.

It was a revelation that held the potential to unravel the tangled web of mystery that had ensnared our town.

And he recalled a distinct scent—a fragrance that had filled the air with an almost tangible presence.

It was an aroma of fruity incense or candy. He'd smelled it when he saw Erin. It was an olfactory marker of the place where he had last seen Ellen, though he couldn't remember where that was.

Christopher's narrative painted a bleak picture of his captivity.

In the beginning, he had been confined to the basement, a place where cockroaches danced on the cold, damp walls. There, Ellen had brought him food and blankets, but she was not his captor. Rather, she was bound in some sort of forced servitude and their fates had simply become intertwined by the cruel hand of Monte.

Together, in the minutes they were able to talk privately, they had dared to hope for freedom beyond the confines of their nightmarish prison, but their dream of escape had been short-lived.

Monte eavesdropped and caught wind of their planned rebellion.

Monte had then dragged Christopher from the basement to the chicken coop—a place that must have felt like a cage within a cage.

In that sinister space, Christopher's life had hung in precarious balance. Each day, as he gazed out through the wire mesh, he wanted to scream out for help, but feared Monte hearing him and cutting his life short. As he slept in the dirt of the coop, the wound to the back of his head began to fester with infection, then the fever set in. He couldn't recall the events that had led him from the chicken coop to the cistern, nor the circumstances surrounding Monte's death. Everything after the basement could only be remembered in short glimpses, like a kaleidoscope bringing shape to flowers, then scattering again between turns.

Chapter Thirty

The desolation stretched out before Alan like a sorrowful hymn, a mournful melody of charred remnants of a smoldering nightmare.

The once-home of Monte lay in ruins. The burnt remains of it stood as a haunting testament to the horrors that had transpired within its embrace.

The skeletal frame of the structure loomed eerily against the twilight, its blackened timbers jutting out like skeletal fingers clawing at the heavens.

Alan moved through the wreckage with a dogged determination, his footsteps stirring up ashes into whisps like restless spirits.

Among the rubble, his keen eyes caught a glimmer of hope-a fragile shard of evidence that hinted at Ellen's presence and confirmed Chris's story.

A scorched bracelet, its metal twisted and warped by the relentless inferno, lay half-buried beneath a mound of ashen debris. It bore her name.

Ellen had been here, trapped within this house of horrors, yet the absence of her body presented a new riddle.

Chapter Thirty-One

Mama and I sat on my bedroom floor, surrounded by a chaotic jumble of old clothes. It was that time of year again-the annual ritual of school shopping and throwing away what no longer fit.

Soon, the chaos of the summer would have to bow to the disciplined cadence of the school year.

Mama's gentle hands expertly sifted through the clothes. She glanced up, noticing the distant expression etched on my face.

It was the sort of look that hinted at profound contemplation, I'm sure-the kind that visited a child on the cusp of discovering the world's deeper complexities.

My fiery red hair, usually tangled from hours of summer play, now lay in a cascade of unruly curls. I'd taken an interest lately in my appearance and had been putting forward a better effort to clean up on a daily basis,

"Mama," I asked. "Do you ever think people really grow out of believing in magic?"

Mama paused her sorting. Her eyes, gentle yet knowing, locked onto mine.

She recognized the weight behind my question-the earnestness of a child grappling with the transition from the innocence of youth to the budding awareness of adulthood.

"Well, Sugar," she replied, her voice soft and comforting. "As folks grow up, they might set aside some of those notions of magic. But that don't mean it ain't real in its own way."

I thought hard about what she was saying as my small fingers unconsciously traced the frayed hem of a faded, animal-print t-shirt that had once been my favorite.

"I understand that, Mama," I said thoughtfully. "Sometimes, as I get older, it feels like there's less magic in the world."

Mama nodded in understanding, looking out the screen door toward the horizon as if seeking wisdom from the setting sun. "Growing up can be like that, Darlin'," she conceded. "But remember, magic ain't just about spells and tricks. It's also in the way a firefly dances on a summer night, or how the stars twinkle up over us and sometimes shoot across the sky. It's all around us, even if we don't see it the same way we used to."

I pondered Mama's words, a sense of reassurance gradually settling over me.

As I looked at the mountain of clothes strewn about us—some worn, others outgrown, each piece holding its own cherished memory—I couldn't help but think about how quickly time had passed.

Each shirt and pair of pants had been a part of my journey- a reminder of the seasons that had come and gone.

The sun cast a soft, amber glow through the window and across my old bedspread. Mama continued sorting through the clothes, methodically folding those that were still serviceable and setting aside the ones that would someday fit Mallory and filing a bag with the ones that had seen their fair share of adventures.

Her hands moved with a practiced grace, a testament to the countless times she had performed this yearly ritual.

I thought about her own lost childhood and wondered out loud. 'Mama.. do you ever miss being a little girl?"

Mama paused, her hands momentarily hovering above a tattered pair of overalls.

She turned her now tearful eyes toward me and a tender smile played at the corners of her lips.

"Oh, honey," she replied, her voice tinged with nostalgia. "There's more to life than being little. Growin' up's fun, too. It's like findin' a new kind of magic—the magic of discoverin' who you're meant to be."

Mama's eyes sparkled as she leaned in a little, seeming to realize that what I really needed was one of her stories.

"Did I ever tell you about the time I saw Big Foot?" she asked.

I giggled and shook my head.

"Well, there was this one time when I was about your age. I was wanderin' through the woods back where I used to live. It was a warm summer evening with fireflies twinklin' all 'round."

She raised her hands and wiggled her fingers, illustrating how the fireflies had twinkled, prompting me to giggle even more.

She smiled and continued.

"As I was walkin' along and then I saw somethin' movin' in the trees. It was big, real big, and covered in shaggy hair from head to toe."

I laughed.

"I'm serious!" she said. "You know he's not scary. He's a great, gentle giant of the woods, who roams around protectin' the creatures of the forest."

"Really?" I squealed, not really believing a word she was saying.

Mama nodded, her eyes holding mine in a captivating gaze. "Yes, Darlin'," she affirmed, "And you know what he did?"

I shook my head.

"He smiled at me," Mama whispered, her voice filled with a sense of wonder. "He had the kindest eyes, like pools of moonlight, and he smiled right at me before disappearin' into the trees."

Chapter Thirty-Two

Adelaide in the summer of '95 was a place where the heat didn't just scorch the Adelaide ground, but it seemed to ignite the very soul of every single one of us that had to walk on it. The air was thick with secrets, and every tree, every shadow, whispered its own version of the truth.

The news folk were like hound dogs on a scent, and when they got wind of that engraved bracelet rising from the ashes and rubble of Monte's old homestead, they couldn't resist the urge to start spinning new yarns over it. It was like a spark in a powder keg, setting' off a frenzy of headlines that proclaimed Ellen dead and the case of the missing Adelaide kids closed – the nightmare in Adelaide was finally over, they said, despite Ellen's mama still sobbing herself to sleep at night and poor Joel no closer to knowing what happened to Ruby.

Despite whatever the news said, though, Alan stayed hard at work. Alan had a sixth sense for trouble. To him, it felt like there was still a storm coming together off beyond the horizon that only he could feel brewin'. He'd seen his share of shit shows in his time, and this ordeal had more twists and turns than a back country road. The newspaper articles might've painted a pretty picture of closure, but Alan wasn't paying none of that silliness any mind.

Ellen, bless her fierce heart, was the kind of girl who could stare danger in the eye without flinching. All her co-workers at Sonic talked about was how tough she was when it came to late-night drunks and creepy customers. Her confetti'd fingernails across the Sonic parking lot stood as testament to that fact, too.

The town might've breathed a sigh of relief, believing we'd closed the book on what became of her, but Alan wasn't ready to turn that final page just yet. In his heart, he thought for sure she'd have fought to the bitter end- and he wasn't so sure Monte's frail little body could have taken her on and won.

Alan thought surely Ellen laid somewhere out in those woods, still fighting. It was just a matter of finding her now.

Secrets had long seemed to sink into the very soil of Adelaide like roots of the ancient timbers that watched over the Pichol Creek woods.

And when you're dealing with secrets, you best believe they don't let go easily.

So, while the headlines declared victory, hailing Charlie and Joel and little Christopher Kendler as heroes and the town carried on with its everyday life, the truth or Ellen's whereabouts and Ruby's demise still remained hidden, like a ghost haunting the woods.

Alan knew it deep in his bones- a few others, like Mama, shared that gnawing suspicion that Ellen might still be out there, fighting for her life and possibly fighting the same monster that had taken Ruby from this world before she ought to have been ready to go.

And that was a monster that might've taken a step back, allowing Monte's death to provide a little cover for the time being, but it sure as shit' hadn't ridden off into the sunset.

It was a tale that'd continue to twist and turn, like the serpentine paths of Pichol Creek, with secrets buried deep in these old Appalachian foothills.

So after the newspapers did their singing, and folks began to settle into a semblance of the old Adelaide normalcy, Alan still couldn't sleep, couldn't rest, until he'd turned over every stone, checked every shadow, and looked into every cave, den, and cistern buried back deep in those hills.

So, one blister in' afternoon, when the muggy summer air was thick enough to cut with a knife, Alan went back out into the woods- alone this time, like a lone wolf prowling its territory. He still had a job to do, and he aimed to see it through.

He scoured those woods, like a man possessed, checking every old well, shed, and junk car he found buried back deep in Monte's property, but came up as empty handed as he'd been when he came in. There were no signs, no clues, nothin' that would lead him closer to the truth.

Frustrated, he headed back toward his car. Then, in the midst of that search, his eyes caught a broken-down Chevy car with the trunk lid popped open a few inches. Hanging out the lid was about ten inches of blonde hair, frayed and wind-twisted with leaves and twigs caught up in it.

"Ellen!" he hollered, running over as quick as he could, tripping over tree roots and buried barbed wire all the way.

When he got there, he threw his fingers under that truck lid and knocked it open with one big heave only to find some life-size rubber doll staring back up at him. No doubt one of Monte's weird hidden treasures- she had a dog leash tied around her neck and her arms sawed off. There was no telling where the weirdo had got her, but she'd been a part of some strange practice, no doubt.

A dead, striped tabby cat lay rotting beside her with a litter of orphaned kittens, huddled together right next to her, weak from starvation, mewing a song of despair.

Though Alan might have been the toughest lawman around, he had a tender heart. He scooped the kittens up, placing them gently in his jacket pockets like fragile treasures.

I reckon maybe he'd just seen enough heartache in those woods, and he wasn't about to let those little souls suffer, too.

Mama, bless her kind heart, was a lot the same way. Rough around the edges, but she, too, was soft on the insides and always trying to save someone.

When Alan brought those kittens to her door, he knew he was bringing them to a haven of compassion and care.

I can still remember him standing at the door,

placing those kittens in that same old fruit box I'd almost tossed my books away in. There were five in total, though the poor little orange colored one didn't make it to the house. Four were left- two striped gray tabbies, a black one, and a little calico.

He asked her if she had any knowin' of how to care for those little ones, suggesting it might keep a certain young someone out of trouble.

Mama turned her eyes toward me, then back at him with a look of grateful realization and said she'd figure it out.

Mama mixed up some warm milk and egg yolk as a temporary cure for their hungry bellies and we fed them real careful from an old plastic straw she pulled out of one of Charlie's Sonic cups in the trash.

Then we put them in that box, in a bed of old rags, in a sunny spot in the kitchen and got our shoes on to head to the library to see what we could find out about helping them further.

For the rest of that summer, those kittens became my purpose as I cared for every one of their needs with a mother's touch.

And though it didn't fix everything- it made a little change in my heart. In those kittens, I found a better understanding of the beauty of hope that can be found in the goodness of another person's heart.

The kind of hope that, in turn, seeds itself in you like a tiny sprout pushing through the earth, reaching for the warmth of the sun.

Chapter Thirty-Three

The story underneath this story is that Kathleen and Alan had a romance brewin' like a slow-cooked stew simmerin' on an old kitchen stove.

It's funny how tragedy can bring two folks together, softening the edges of an otherwise stern man and melting the resolve of a tough woman.

So, as it was, on that day, with the sun hangin' high in the sky, casting a golden glow over Adelaide, they found themselves standing at the sheriff station, locked in a moment that seemed to stretch on forever.

The weight of the summer, the disappearances, the heartache-it all hung heavy in the air between 'em, but it had come time for Kathleen to head on out.

Kathleen had been through the ringer in them woods, facing horrors that'd haunt her for a lifetime, but she'd also found something unexpected with Alan. Theirs was a bond forged in the fires of adversity, and in the midst of the uncertainty that shrouded the disappearances of Ruby and Ellen, their hearts had found solace in each other's company.

When the order came in from Richmond, Kathleen knew it was time to say her goodbyes and it was a hard farewell.

The kind that tugs at your heartstrings and leaves you with a lump in your throat.

She knew that Alan wouldn't ever leave Adelaide until he unraveled the mystery of what had become of Ruby, and that that might not be ever- so she didn't bother asking him.

State police had decided that there was nothing linking the disappearance of Ellen Dewey to that of Ruby Milton. They declared Ellen likely dead and closed the case on her, letting Ruby's sit as cold as it had been the night Brian Dewey had to settle without his french fries.

As Kathleen and Alan stood there together, the quiet hum of the old light fixture humming at them like an old lullaby, they made an agreement of sorts.

Kathleen would go back to her life for now, but she'd come visit on the weekends if Alan would have her.

And of course he would.

It was a strange little love story now writ in the pages of Adelaide history.

As Kathleen and Alan stood there, a bond formed in the crucible of Adelaide's darkest days, they knew that this was far from the end of the tale they'd someday tell, holding hands in their old rockers together on some quiet front porch in some other reality than the one they stood in then.

And, yet, when Kathleen looked into Alan's eyes, she saw the doubt that clouded his thoughts.

A woman who understood him less might have thought he was doubting her, but Kathleen knew better.

He was holding onto a nagging feeling, like an itch he couldn't quite reach, that something about Ellen's vanishing and Monte's death still didn't quite add up- that beneath the surface, there was a whole other darkness yet to be unveiled.

After all, everyone else including the state bureau of investigations had plum turned their eyes away from the fact that, after Monte did whatever he did, someone had shot and killed him, then dragged his ass back to the creek to dump it.

Someone knew more than they let on.

Yet, everyone else seemed content to just let whoever that was get away with it. Like killing Monte absolved them of anything else they might have played some part in.

"You know, Kathleen," Alan said. "It still just feels like this whole mess was tied up too quick. There's someone else out there- I don't know why they're in such a hurry to pull you back out of here with another suspect somewhere on the loose. This is too neat. Nothing ties up this neat when there's murder involved."

Kathleen replied with a somber tone. "Neat?" she asked. "Alan, people died, lives were shattered, and families torn apart. There ain't nothin' neat about any of this. It's a mess, a tragedy that's scarred this town deep and no we don't have all the answers. We probably never will. But sometimes you have to decide to set something down so you can walk off and heal from it."

She stepped closer to him, looking at him with a deep intensity, "But I get it. You're a good man, and good men can't stand to leave stones unturned, no matter how much worse they might uncover- no matter how hot those stones are or how badly they're gonna burn. It's admirable."

Then, Kathleen's gaze softened, and she added, "But you need to remember, Alan, every time you peel back a layer in this darkness, the one underneath might be twice as rotten. You gotta be prepared for what you might find. Are you ready for that- to cast the weight of even more sorrow on this town?"

Alan's eyes met hers, and he took a deep breath, considering what she was saying. He knew she was right. He knew that uncovering the truth could unleash more pain and turmoil on the good folks of Adelaide.

But deep down, he couldn't shake the feeling that something was amiss. Something still lurked in the shadows, waiting to be brought to light.

With a heavy sigh, he finally spoke.

"You're right, Honey. It might get messier before it gets clearer, and I can't guarantee that the truth will bring comfort to anyone. In fact, it's probably going to do the opposite. But I can't just stand by and let whatever it is keep on festering. I owe it to this town-to those kids- to find out what really happened. Even if it means more pain."

Kathleen nodded, her eyes reflecting a mix of understanding and respect.

She planted one more sweet kiss on him, then hurried out of the station, intent to be a mile down the road before she let her first tears fall.

Chapter Thirty-Four

The summer heat had mellowed, and with Monte the pervert now dead, Mama let the woods call me back with their sweet, earthy allure.

I had my basket of kittens with me, and I felt a sense of freedom coursing through my veins. The troubles of my young life and the filthy secrets that hung like heavy clouds over Adelaide were momentarily forgotten as I ventured toward Pichol Creek.

The kittens were crawling and swatting and ready to play. I thought they might like to see the minnows and dragonflies that lurk around the edges of the shallow brown water.

So there by Pichol Creek, I stood, the kittens at my feet with their tiny eyes wide in wonder as they stalked at the grasshoppers and little frogs that danced in the golden light. The creek gurgled a gentle lullaby to the woods and I took a deep breath, letting it all fill my lungs.

Then, something caught my eye – bare footprints, fresh as morning dew, imprinted in the muddy banks.

People footprints.

Bigger than mine, probably smaller than Mama's.

They ran from the water's edge, up the bank,

and into the tall grass, as if someone had rushed from the creek in a hurry.

I looked all over the creek bed, though, and something peculiar stuck out to me.

The footprints had come out of the water- but I couldn't see any place where they'd gone in.

They were far apart and I remembered one time when I'd gone hunting with Charlie and Joel that Joel had told me footprints spaced wide like that usually mean something was running.

I gathered up my kittens and put them back in their basket, shutting the lid, then I followed the trail of footprints into the tall grass, guided by my own curiosity. I weaved through the underbrush as the rustling leaves and distant bird songs laid a peaceful soundtrack to my strange pursuit.

The deeper into the woods I got, though, the footprints became more erratic, like the person who'd left them was in a hurry- almost frantic- and stumbling all over themselves.

The kittens were restless, too. Their mewls were growing' more anxious as we delved further into the unknown.

The idea of a changeling crossed my mind, but I quickly shook that fear away. Changelings were said to be creatures of mischief- tricksters who swapped themselves for human babies. They were bound to the land, tied to the hearth and home. They were not creatures of the water.

I pondered what kind of being might have left these prints, what sort of creature could be water-bound and yet leave no trace of its entry into the creek.

All I knew was it couldn't be human..

Soon, I lost sight of the footprints entirely. Like whatever it was had simply vanished into thin air, or taken on some other form.

My heart raced, and I couldn't help but feel like I was treading on the edge of something profound- something that defied the laws of nature.

Finally, I thought, I'd found my proof of something not human living back in those woods.

*Sourwood Mountain Tales - **Tess, Book Two: Nereid** by Jenni Lorraine*

Chapter Thirty-Five

As Joel walked into the sheriff station to talk to Alan, the air grew thick with a hostile tension as if the furniture itself was aware of the turbulence that still lay between the two men.

Alan sat at his desk, barely noticing as Joel walked in, rapping lightly on the door facing.

"Sheriff Cline?" he asked, grabbing Alan's attention.

Alan looked up, a little startled, and scooted back in his chair to a standing position, reaching across his desk to shake Joel's hand.

"Haven't seen you lately, Joel," Alan said, friendly. "How you been? Have a seat. What brings you?"

Joel cleared his throat and nervously approached the chair, taking a seat.

"Sheriff," he began, his voice steady but tinged with a hint of bitterness. "I reckon it's high time we cleared the air between us."

Alan looked up, his eyes meeting Joel's with a wariness.

Joel cleared his throat again and continued. "You and I both know the accusations that were thrown around back when you found that old ax. I ain't sayin' I didn't do nothing wrong. I think about that dog all the time and can't believe what I did, but all this time I've been thinking hard about the way you were so sure I had something to do with Ruby and I just.. There's something I need to say. I want you to know somethin'."

Alan leaned back in his chair, silently urging Joel to continue. He wasn't sure what Joel had come to talk to him about- but he knew that a man like Joel didn't open up easy. Whatever it was mattered.

"I loved Ruby," Joel cried, his voice cracking with emotion. "More than I ever thought I could love anyone-And had she told me about that baby, I would have stood by her. I'd have helped her raise it, no matter whose child it was."

The weight of Joel's words hung in the air heavy.. He continued, each uttered sentence carrying the weight of years of guilt and heartache.

"I know you thought I had something to do with her dying, Sheriff, but I swear on all that's holy, I would've protected her and that baby with everything I had. What I did to that poor dog was wrong- but I did it in a blind fury because he'd gnawed on her. I'd like to know who killed her because I'd do the same to them without flinching. I guess what I'm saying is I need you to keep looking, Sheriff. I need you to find the son of a bitch because if you don't, and I figure it out first, I swear there's gonna be more bloodshed. I feel it's only right to warn you."

Alan's stony expression softened as he listened to Joel's tearful plea.

He finally spoke, his voice laced with remorse.

"Joel, I... I should've known better. I should've believed in your innocence from the start. I let my doubts and maybe a little bit of an over-eagerness to get this case closed cloud my judgment, and for that, I'm truly sorry."

Joel nodded. "We both made mistakes, Sheriff. I can forgive you for all that. But I won't ever forgive you if you just let Ruby be forgotten like the rest of the town's trying to do."

As they sat there, two men burdened by the past, the scars of Adelaide's darkest days ran deep, but in that moment, the healing had begun, and the weight on their hearts felt a little lighter.

Joel's gaze remained fixed on the worn wooden floorboards as he thought about Ruby. The room seemed to grow heavy with the weight of his deepest regrets.

"If only I'd have known she was pregnant, I'd have married her," he muttered, his voice laden with sorrow. "Maybe she'd still be alive today."

Alan leaned forward, resting his forearms on his desk. "Joel," he began gently. "There's something you need to know. Ruby... she wasn't the motherly type. She didn't want to be tied down by a child. She wanted to be free."

Joel's head snapped up, his eyes locking onto Alan's. "You didn't know her, Cline."

Alan hesitated for a moment, choosing his words carefully.

"There was another baby, Joel. Before this one, Ruby was pregnant once before. Before she even knew you, I reckon. She gave it up for adoption in Nashville."

Joel's eyes narrowed in confusion. "That ain't true," he said, shaking his head. "She would have told me if there was something like that. She never mentioned no baby to me in all the time we were together. We told each other everything."

Alan sighed, his gaze distant as he thought back on the trip to Nashville and the interview with the adoption agency rep.

"Ruby didn't want that life, Joel," He said. "She wanted to leave and start fresh. She wanted to move to Nashville and chase her dreams. It's a long story, but she came up on this outfit out of Nashville and they took the baby for her. They found it another family. She signed her rights off and pretended it never happened. Her and Dickie Kendler. He took her down there. It was his baby. This last one likely was, too."

Joel's shoulders sagged with the weight of this newfound revelation. "I see," he murmured, staring blankly at the floor.

As the two men sat in contemplative silence, Alan's thoughts drifted back to his conversation with Charlie. He remembered the hushed tones, the exchange of money, and the secrecy that surrounded Ruby's departure from Adelaide. He thought about telling Joel about that part of the story, too.

Instead, he chose to keep that part of the story to himself, not wanting to sow discord between the brothers.

Joel finally broke the silence, his voice heavy with emotion as he stood up from the chair, preparing to leave and head on home. "Thank you, Sheriff. For tellin' me the truth."

Alan nodded, a sense of closure settling over them both.

"Joel, we've all made mistakes along the way. It's time we put the past behind us and find a way to move forward. Nobody around here doubts your love for Ruby. Everyone I've talked to about the two of y'all has told me how devoted you were to her. She's gone, though. I'll do everything I can to bring whoever hurt her to justice, but you need to leave it to me. Put it behind yourself or it's going to rot your heart something awful."

Joel nodded, sliding his old worn ball cap back on his head, smoothing down his dark curls.

"Let it. I ain't got much use for it now anyway."

Chapter Thirty-Six

Over the following days, the creaking of Alan's old wooden chair beneath him was a familiar companion, accompanying him on countless late-night re-readings of Ruby's case file.

The file itself bore the scars of his and Kathleen's countless readings, its edges softened by dog-ears and wear. Each page held a fragment of a story that had sent shockwaves through Adelaide, then wound up forgotten like a body rotting away in the thickets.

As Alan thumbed through the pages, re-reading everything they'd managed to gather piece- by- piece, he stumbled upon something he'd never read before.

Kathleen had written a new statement for the file, only days before Christopher had been found. It was the re-telling of the wild story Erik and I had shared with her about seeing Steven in the woods, covered in blood- and about her conversation with Steven afterward.

Alan's fingers traced the lines of her words, engrossed in every word he was reading.

She'd told him about talking to Steven and that Steven had acted fishy, but he'd brushed it off in the moment. He knew Steven's secret about liking men. He figured with all the rigamarole going on, it made sense that Steven would get nervous.

He also knew that I had a wild imagination and that Erik would go along with just about anything I said.

The whole event had been quickly brushed off into a pile of possible clues that were also possibly nothing, then forgotten about in the excitement of Christopher's rescue.

In the hazy heat of that summer, it had been easy to overlook such a detail. It was just one weird story in a heap of weird stories. Adelaide had been a town in turmoil, rocked by tragedy and uncertainty.

But now, with the passage of time and the weight of responsibility back solely on his shoulders, Alan recognized the importance of Kathleen's report.

He knew he needed to speak with Steven again- to revisit that night when me and Erik had glimpsed Steven's alarming condition out there in the woods.

As he read the report, Alan was visited by another recollection.

The memory of Steven's red pickup truck flickered in Alan's mind, much like the intermittent flashes of lightning during a summer storm. It had been a fleeting detail, easily dismissed at the time. The Red Scottsdale lead had gone nowhere because, as was pointed out to him, they were in wild abundance in Adelaide and the surrounding area, after all.

But now, as he delved deeper into the

labyrinthine clues of Ruby's case, that piece of the puzzle held newfound significance.

The surveillance footage from the night Ellen was taken had revealed the ominous presence of a red Scottsdale pickup truck, though most of it including any view of the driver's seat had been hidden under a spider web that obstructed the camera's view.

The now overlapping threads of coincidence demanded another look.

Adelaide had always been a place where secrets hid in plain sight, where neighbors harbored hidden truths, and where the past had a way of resurfacing when least expected.

Suddenly, Steven came cruising right back into the list of potential suspects behind the wheel of that old red Scottsdale.

As the pieces of the puzzle fell into place, a chilling revelation coursed through Alan's mind like a shock of ice-cold water on a July evening.

The memory of Christopher's words- his mention of sweet candy smells-suddenly made perfect sense.

It was a jigsaw of scent and memory that formed an ominous picture.

In the haze of recollection, Alan's mind drifted back to the day of Ruby's funeral, when Steven had lost his proverbial shit during the eulogy and poor Alan had been forced to drive him home.

On the way home, Steven had asked for a light, then helped himself to a grape cigarillo right there in Alan's car.

It had seemed inconsequential at the time, merely a minor detail in the grand scheme of things, but Alan had taken note of the scent- a sickly sweet smell shrouding a puff of noxious smoke that lingered in his squad car for days afterward.

Now, that seemingly insignificant detail took on a sinister form. The pieces of the puzzle aligned with eerie precision, spelling out a grim truth that he could no longer deny.

Steven had quite likely played a role in this nightmarish scenario- a role that had remained concealed thus far.

As the evening shadows lengthened, Alan made up his mind to re-visit Christopher in the morning armed with a pack of grape cigarillos.

And, sure enough, come morning, he ventured to the Kendler house. Christopher had been released from the hospital and was resting at home, but Debbie had not let him take any visitors yet. Word was that he was still mighty rattled by it all.

Debbie answered the door, her expression a mixture of curiosity and apprehension. Alan greeted her with a nod.

"Debbie, could you bring Christopher out to the porch, please?" he requested, his voice steady but laced with an urgency that Debbie couldn't deny.

Moments later, Christopher emerged from the house. He could barely walk, so he was hanging onto his Mama, but he looked up at the Sheriff and smiled.

"Good to see you!" he said. "Doctor says I'll be able to ride my bike again soon. Mama said she's going to get me a brand new one on her next paycheck!"

Alan nodded. "That's great, Buddy," he said. "Listen, I need to ask you to help me. It might not be fun, but it's very important. Can I count on you?"

Christopher looked at him, confused, but nodded.

Not wasting another minute, Alan lit up one of the grape cigarillos, letting a thin wisp of aromatic smoke curl into the morning breeze..

"Christopher," Alan began, his voice gentle but purposeful, "I need you to tell me what you smell." He extended the cigarillo towards Christopher's face. The scent, so seemingly innocuous, wafted towards Christopher, and in that moment, the past collided with the present.

Christopher's reaction was immediate and visceral. The scent of the grape cigarillo triggered an overwhelming surge of fear and panic. His eyes widened in terror, and his breathing quickened, shallow and erratic. Unbidden tears welled up in his eyes, streaming down his cheeks as he turned, burying his face in his mother's belly.

Alan's heart ached as he watched

Christopher's distress unfold before him. He hadn't anticipated such a powerful reaction and it left him torn between feeling guilty and feeling determined.

"Easy, Christopher," Alan whispered, his voice soothing and steady. He gently withdrew the cigarillo and extinguished it, allowing the fragrant smoke to dissipate as he reached his free hand for Christopher's back, giving it a gentle pat.

"I'm so sorry," he murmured, his empathy palpable. "I didn't mean to upset you like this."

Debbie, confused and horrified by what she had just witnessed, didn't know what to say. She just looked Alan in the eyes, furious, and gave a simple, polite command.

"Sheriff," she said. "I believe it's time for you to go."

Chapter Thirty-Seven

Charlie leaned in, his rugged face drawn close to inspect the footprints in the mud alongside me.

His experienced eyes, weathered by years of wandering these woods, squinted thoughtfully as he examined the mysterious tracks etched in the soft, damp earth. The lines on his furrowed brow deepened with each passing second, a clear sign of his growing intrigue.

"Well, now," he muttered, his voice tinged with a hint of bewilderment. "These here tracks are mighty peculiar, ain't they?"

I nodded eagerly, my young eyes wide with wonder and my heart pounding with excitement. The footprints before us were unlike any I had ever seen. They seemed to materialize out of thin air, as if some invisible being had briefly touched our world and left its elusive mark.

Charlie's calloused fingers traced the outline of one of the prints, his hands seasoned by countless hours spent in these very woods.

His words carried the weight of wisdom as he spoke. "Seems like these tracks just come outta nowhere, don't they? Just walked up out of the water like a toad or something without ever going into it. And I'll be damned if I can figure out where they lead."

I admired Charlie's knowledge and experience. He was the one person I knew who might hold the key to unlocking the secrets of this particular mystery. Together, we crouched beside the gurgling creek, our eyes glued to the ground, as if the answers we sought were written in the patterns of the gravel itself.

As I watched Charlie ponder the inexplicable footprints, a sense of awe washed over me. The world felt different in those moments, as if we had stumbled upon something that transcended the boundaries of our ordinary existence. There was a blend of curiosity, wonder, and just a hint of unease coursing through me.

When we got back to the house, I listened intently from the other room as Mama's hushed voice mingled with Charlie's low tones. Their conversation filled with a sense of intrigue and concern. It was clear that they were just as baffled by the strange footprints as I was.

I fed my kittens in the hallway where I could eavesdrop better, my gaze shifting between their tiny hungry mews and the door to the living room.

Mama's voice, tinged with a mixture of curiosity and worry, reached my ears. "Someone washed down the creek, Charlie, then crawled out. That's the only thing it could be. Do you think it might have been the Dewey girl?"

Charlie's response was measured as he considered Mama's question.

"It's hard to say, Jo. But whoever left them tracks didn't come from nowhere close by and the creek gets real shallow just up flow from where they are. I don't think a person could have washed through there. I know for sure a boat couldn't."

With my kittens snuggled in my arms, I watched and listened, waiting for any sign that Mama and Charlie might figure out, together, what had happened out there at Pichol Creek.

It never came.

So, with nothing else to be done about it, I decided for myself that I'd just have to head back to the library and do my own research.

Chapter Thirty-Eight

Meanwhile, Alan was on a mission, determined to figure out Steven's involvement in Christopher's kidnapping.

Already knowing that Steven had been evasive and refused to talk to Kathleen, Alan decided to come with back-up for a second conversation.

He led the charge, his jaw set with steely resolve, while two of his trusted deputies trailed behind like wary hounds on the hunt.

Inside that house, Steven waited, his stomach churnin' like an old washing machine. He'd heard on the police scanner that they were heading his way and he didn't bother trying to run.

He loaded his shotgun and sat behind the front door. Fear, anger, and guilt swirled within him and he'd become a trapped animal, caught between desperation and defiance.

As the lawmen closed in on Steven's house, tension of all that had happened hung thick in the air, and the weight of the impending confrontation bore down on them all, hinting at the reckoning awaiting.

In the tapestry of this whole story, it's this scene that remains most vivid-a snapshot frozen in the annals of Adelaide history.

Alan and his deputies cautiously approached Steven's house. They moved slowly, each step calculated and deliberate.

As they neared the house, a sudden, deafening crack split the air. The sharp report of a gunshot echoed through the neighborhood, sending startled mothers into a frenzy of gathering their babies up and rushing inside.

The deputies instinctively dropped to the ground, taking cover behind their cars. Each of their hearts was pounding in their chests as their eyes darted back and forth between each other, none of them quite knowing what to do.

Though Alan's pulse raced, he remained standing, his eyes fixed on the house. Another gunshot followed, then a third.

The bullets whizzed dangerously close, impacting the ground with sharp, biting cracks. It was clear that Steven was not going down without a fight.

"Steven!" Alan shouted, his voice carrying over the chaos. "We just want to talk! Lower your weapon, and we can get through this peacefully!"

There was no response, only the oppressive silence that seemed to settle over the neighborhood like a heavy shroud. Alan's mind raced as he weighed his options. He knew that any wrong move could escalate the situation further, and he was determined to bring this standoff to a peaceful end.

For what felt like an eternity, they remained in a tense stalemate, each side unwilling to give ground. Alan's deputies maintained their positions, their weapons trained on the house, ready to respond to any threat. The sun dipped lower on the horizon, signaling that time was dragging on too long. They needed to get this wrapped up.

Just as hope began to wane, a voice called out from inside the house. It was shaky and uncertain, carrying a note of desperation.

"I didn't do it, Sheriff. You gotta believe me."

It was Steven.

Alan could hear the tremor in his voice and saw an opportunity.

"Steven, we can talk about this," Alan replied, keeping his voice calm and measured. "Nobody's hurt. We're all just fine out here. You haven't done anything too bad yet, so let's just talk this out before it gets worse than it needs to be. You need to put down your weapon and come out slowly. We're here to help."

There was a long, agonizing pause, during which Alan held his breath. Then, slowly and hesitantly, the front door of the house creaked open, revealing Steven's silhouette in the fading light.

But he didn't come out.

"I'll talk to you," he said. "But you have to come in here."

Alan's thoughts raced. All his training told him not to comply with such a request.

But he thought of Joel crying at his desk. He thought of Ruby Milton laying dead and forgotten in the creek bed. He thought of little Christopher Kendler curled up and near death at the bottom of that cistern.

And he thought of Ellen. Still lost. Her only hope for coming home rested in whatever information Alan could dig up before she reached an untimely end of her own.

He gave his deputies a long, apologetic glance.

Then he walked into the house and shut the door behind him.

Chapter Thirty-Nine

Steven paced in the dining room of his house, still holding his gun in his hand as he waved his hands around, gesturing wildly as he tried to explain.

"I... I never meant for her to be hurt," Steven stammered, his eyes filled with remorse. "Me and Monte were needing some cash and I mentioned that the Deweys had all kinds of cash.. And Brian's always in trouble. I told Monte if we take the girl and talk about Brian's trouble in the note, they won't go to the cops. They'll do what we say. We'll get a pay day out of it.. And with everything going on with Ruby it was a good time to do it too. We'd both already been looked at and cleared, right? You'd leave us alone... But Monte... he went too far with it. It's my fault. I should've known he would..."

Alan listened intently, his own anger and frustration simmering beneath the surface. He knew he was finally getting closer to at least some of the answers he had been seeking.

"We had her out there at his house.. I came out one day and caught him on top of her.. He... he threatened to expose me," Steven continued, his voice trembling. "We... we had a thing together, Sheriff. But Monte didn't care about me.. And he didn't care if anyone knew what he was. He didn't care about anything. He said he'd ruin me if I ever told anyone what I saw him do to Ellen."

The revelation sent a shiver down Alan's spine, the complexity of the situation becoming painfully clear. Secrets and hidden relationships had woven a web of deceit that had culminated in a horrific scene.

"And Christopher?" Alan pressed, his voice steady despite his fury.

Steven's gaze dropped, his face contorted with regret. "I knew Monte needed to be stopped when he took Christopher. I... I couldn't let him hurt another innocent child. I told him we just needed to let them both go. He never sent the note. He never did what he said he would do. He just wanted them. He wanted the kids. I helped him grab Ellen because I thought it was a money thing. I never would have. And I didn't know nothing about Christopher til I got out there and he had him tied up down in the basement. I don't think he ever touched him, though. I hope he didn't."

Before more could be said, a sudden, deafening gunshot rang out from outside the house. Startled, Alan and Steven both turned toward the window, their hearts pounding.

Through the shattered glass, they could see a rookie deputy. His face was etched with panic, standing with a smoking gun in hand.

His misguided attempt to end the standoff had only escalated the situation further.

"Get down!" Alan shouted, pushing Steven to the floor just as another shot pierced the air. Bullets whizzed through the room, shattering picture frames and splintering furniture.

Steven fired a shot back out the window in a panic.

Chaos erupted as the deputies returned fire, their shots ringing out in the confined space.

In the midst of the chaos, a searing pain tore through Alan's shoulder, causing him to cry out. He clutched the wound, his vision swimming as he struggled to maintain his composure.

The gunfire continued, and the room became a nightmarish battleground. Steven, trapped in the crossfire, was struck by a bullet and fell to the floor, his life gone in an instant.

The shootout ended as quickly as it had begun. As Steven's body hit the hardwood with a thud, the deafening silence that followed marked the weight of a new tragedy.

Alan, wounded and reeling, knew that their pursuit of the truth was far from over.

Outside, the approaching sirens grew louder, and the flashing lights of emergency vehicles pierced the growing darkness as summy storm clouds gathered overhead.

As Alan was attended to by the deputies and the chaos began to subside, one question still loomed large in his mind—where in the hell was Ellen?

Chapter Forty

It was a couple of days after the shootout when Alan, recovering in the hospital, received an unexpected visitor.

Artie Milton, the father of Ruby, sauntered into that sterile hospital room with a weighty presence that matched the oppressive stench of his morning drunk. Artie was a man weathered by years of hardship and addiction, his scruffy beard framing a grizzled face that had seen more trouble than most.

He was a portly figure in tattered clothes. His body bore the telltale signs of a life long lived with a bottle as his closest companion. His haggard appearance stood in stark contrast to the clean, white walls of the hospital room, but his eyes held a certain resignation- a weariness that comes from relentless grief and guilt.

Kathleen sat at Alan's bedside, holding his hand in hers as Artie approached.

"Darlin'," Alan said, barely louder than a whisper. "This is Artie Milton. He's Ruby's father."

Kathleen's eyes turned back to Artie, wide and full of surprise.

"It's nice to meet you," she said, unsure yet if it were true.

Artie shuffled closer to the bedside. His heavy breaths punctuated every hefty step.

Finally, standing at the foot of the bed, his weathered fingers fidgeted with the edge of his tattered jacket as he found the strength to speak, a heaviness in his voice that mirrored the weight of his words.

"I just wanted to come here and tell you that it's okay, Sheriff," he murmured, his words carrying the weight of a thousand regrets. "You can stop lookin' for Ruby's killer, if that's what you want. In fact, you ought to. It ain't gonna change nothin'."

His eyes met Alan's. There was a profound sadness in that exchange- a shared understanding of the perceived futility of Alan's pursuit.

Artie had lost his daughter, and the truth behind her death remained buried beneath the unforgiving grit of Pichol Creek.

"It will make a difference," Alan said. "I'm going to get justice for that girl."

"Sometimes, Sheriff, you just gotta let things be. Some secrets, they're meant to stay buried. Ain't nothin' we can do to change that now," Artie said. "All that's ever come from trying to figure any of this out is more and more people dying. Just let it go. If you have to find someone to blame, you blame it on me. I didn't do a good enough job with her. I didn't even know she was gone. Seems like a father ought to have felt something, you know? A change in his heart or something somehow. A man ought to just know when his baby's heart stops beating. You'd think so, anyway."

Sheriff Alan, lying in that hospital bed, still bearing the wounds from the recent shootout with Steven, listened intently to Artie's weary words. The heaviness of Artie's presence filled the room, and the weight of his grief seemed to hang in the air like a dense fog.

But although he understood the depths of Artie's pain, Alan also knew that there was an even greater responsibility at play—the responsibility to seek justice for Ruby and for all those whose lives had been forever changed by the mysteries of that summer.

With a firm resolve, Alan responded, his voice unwavering despite his injuries. "I appreciate your words, Artie, and I understand your pain. But the town can't rest until Ruby does. I made a promise to find the truth, and I intend to keep it."

Chapter Forty-One

Me and Erik had been hunkered down in front of that old CRT television for what felt like a lifetime, our fingers flying across those chunky gray controllers as we took on the pixelated adventures of Super Mario and his pals. It was a sweltering summer day-the kind that made the air heavy and thick- and we'd been chasing' digital mushrooms and stompin' on Goombas for over two hours straight under the air conditioning vent, committed to not feeling a second of it.

Just when we thought we could go on boppin' and jumpin' our way through the Mushroom Kingdom forever, Erik's mom barged in with her no-nonsense look, hands on her hips like a stern schoolmarm. She'd seen us glued to that TV screen long enough, and she wasn't having none of it.

"Y'all have been at those video games for a while now," she said, her voice laced with a mix of concern and annoyance. "You best find somethin' else to do before you turn into them plumbers yourselves."

We knew she was right, and as we reluctantly powered down that Nintendo, I dreaded going back outside. I could already feel the sweat clinging to my back like a wet rag.

"I ain't playing outside today," I said as we made our way out the front door. "We just need to find somewhere else to go."

"You got pool money?" Erik asked.

I shook my head sadly.

He nodded.

"Me, either," he said. Lying. Erik always had money.

We grabbed our bikes and pedaled through town with the sun beating down on our backs like it had a bone to pick with us.

The streets stretched out in front of us, each one holding its own secrets and stories. The smell of freshly cut grass mingled with the distant hum of cicadas, and the whole place felt like it was caught in a never-ending summer haze.

As we coasted along, the wind whistling in our ears, I turned to Erik and decided it was as good a time as any to share what had been nagging' at my mind.

"Erik," I said. "You remember that day down by Pichol Creek, don't ya?"

He nodded. "Yeah, What 'bout it?"

I felt a flutter of excitement as I spilled the beans. "Well, I saw somethin' down there-something' strange. Footprints, Erik, but not just any footprints. These were like nothin' I'd ever seen. I even showed Charlie and he couldn't figure it out, either."

Erik's curiosity was piqued, and he gave me a sideways glance as we pedaled side by side. "What do you mean, strange?"

I told the tale as we rode, describing the prints that seemed to come out of nowhere, leading up the muddy banks of the creek without a trace of where they'd come from or where they ended.

He nodded, contemplating what I'd told him.

"Well, Tess, if the footprints are as weird as you say, maybe we oughta head to the library. Could be one of your monsters. Plus, the library has air conditioning, so why not just hang out there?"

I grinned. "Erik, that's exactly what we oughta do! You're a genius!"

So, a few minutes later, me and Erik were huddled together in that dusty old library like a pair of detectives on a mighty important case. The air was thick with the smell of ancient books and the only sounds were the soft rustling of pages and the distant tick-tock of the old clock.

And it was on that day that we came to learn about the Rusalki- a mysterious water spirit that we reckoned might hold the key to the strange footprints I'd found down by Pichol Creek.

If the illustrations were to be believed,

Rusalkis were cute as bugs, but treacherous as the creek after a heavy rain.

The tales told of their knack for beguiling poor souls who happened upon them. Folklore said they could step out of the water and walk as humans on land, weaving their charms wherever they roamed.

As I read those words, Erik's eyes grew as wide as full moons and a shiver danced down my spine.

Finally, we'd found what we were looking for.

Chapter Forty-Two

Alan had finally been given the all-clear to leave that sterile, white-walled hospital room. As he stepped out into the warm embrace of the southern sun, he took a deep breath of freedom.

It felt good to be out of those hospital gowns and back in his own clothes, even if they were wrinkled and crumpled from days of disuse.

He climbed into his cruiser, which he'd insisted be parked and waiting for him, and the familiar scent of worn leather and aged coffee cups hugged him like an old friend.

The town of Adelaide had never looked more beautiful. Its streets meandered through the rolling foothills of Virginia. It was a place where everyone knew everyone else's business, except when they didn't, and that was his job to work out.

He was needed there. His presence made a difference. And he was back- present- in his role after several days of rest.

With a sense of purpose, he drove straight to the sheriff's station. The routine of his job was a welcome comfort. He was eager to catch up on all that he'd missed while confined to that hospital bed.

Just as he settled into his desk and fired up his old computer, the phone rang. The shrill ring cut through the stillness of the station, and he reached for the receiver.

"Alan Cline here," he said as he answered, his voice steady and professional.

"Alan, it's Marty Schrein at the state lab," came the voice on the other end, sharp and to the point. Alan smiled, thankful he was able to take this call. It was important.

He leaned forward, his heart rate quickening. "What have you got?" he asked

The last several weeks had seemed to drag on as the lab processed the evidence found at Monte's burnt-out house. Now, the answers were finally here.

"We analyzed every item you sent," Marty said. "We looked at every bone fragment, every piece of jewelry, and every suspicious substance. The results are all the same- nothing you sent us is human."

"So that means?" Alan asked, already sure of the answer.

"Nobody died in that fire, sir," Marty said.

"Thank you," Alan said, unable to say more. He laid the phone back on the receiver and stared, blankly, at the food.

Alan had spent countless sleepless nights poring over reports, trying to make sense of it all. Even after the news reporters were content to say Ellen died in that fire, Alan couldn't escape the nagging feeling that there was more to the story- that somehow Ellen Dewey had slipped through her kidnappers' grasp.

And now, armed with the findings of the state lab, he felt certain.

Ellen Dewey was still alive.

LOOK FOR PART 3

RUSALKI

New Year's Day, 2024

Milton Keynes UK
Ingram Content Group UK Ltd.
UKHW020255221123
432980UK00018B/1344

9 798885 263191